THE LINE

Where Responsibility Stops

BOOK ONE

A Novel

J.L. BLOCK ENTERPRISES

LAMPERT & SONS PUBLISHING

Copyright

THE LINE: Where Responsibility Stops

Publisher: Lampert & Sons Publishing

Author: J.L. Block Enterprises

Paperback Edition

ISBN: 978-1-969709-67-8

Hardcover Edition

ISBN: 978-1-969709-68-5

First Edition: January 2026

Printed in the United States of America

10 9 8 7 6 5 4 3 2 1

For Tootsie, who survived the first draft.

For Theodore, who remains unimpressed.

And for everyone who holds the line.

AUTHORS' FOREWORD

A Note from Justin Lampert & Erik Block

Dear Reader,

What you hold in your hands is a lie.

Well, not a *lie* exactly. More of a... heavily sanitized truth. A truth that has been sanded down, buffed up, and wrapped in enough legal disclaimers to satisfy the twenty-three different agencies across nine countries who reviewed this manuscript before allowing it anywhere near a printing press.

The stories contained within are based on actual operations. We want to be absolutely clear about that. Every mission described actually happened. Every person we encountered was real. Every line we held was held exactly as depicted.

But the *details* have been changed.

Significantly.

Catastrophically, some might say.

You see, we originally wrote this book the way things actually occurred—the unvarnished, unredacted, nothing-held-back account of what we do and how we do it. We thought the world deserved to know the truth.

We were wrong.

The first draft was 1,247 pages. It contained operational details that, according to our legal team, would have "immediately collapsed four NATO alliances, destabilized the global banking system, triggered no fewer than three separate wars, and caused at least one head of state to have what they diplomatically called 'a complete psychological episode.'"

We thought they were being dramatic.

Then we showed the manuscript to Tootsie.

For those unfamiliar, Tootsie is our Siberian tiger.

Yes, we have a pet Siberian tiger. No, we will not explain how we acquired him. The paperwork alone would require its own redacted appendix. His name is not negotiable—Erik chose it during a moment of what he now describes as "temporary

3

humanity," and Erik does not reverse decisions.

Tootsie is, by any objective measure, one of the most dangerous apex predators currently in private ownership. He weighs 673 pounds. He has survived encounters that we cannot legally discuss. He once made eye contact with a grizzly bear, and the grizzly bear *apologized*. He is, according to three separate wildlife experts, "the single most intimidating land mammal they have ever personally witnessed."

He is also, for reasons we don't entirely understand, absolutely terrified of the vacuum cleaner. But that's beside the point.

Tootsie does not frighten easily.

We gave him the original manuscript to review. (Don't ask why—it's a security protocol involving scent-based authentication that we developed after the Incident in Helsinki.) He sniffed the pages. He read approximately four paragraphs—Tootsie is surprisingly literate for a tiger, though his literary criticism tends toward the visceral rather than the analytical.

Then he passed out.

Cold.

Out.

Six hundred and seventy-three pounds of apex predator, collapsed on our living room floor, rendered unconscious by the sheer intensity of what we had written.

When he woke up three hours later, he refused to enter that room for two weeks. He still won't look directly at our filing cabinet.

That's when we knew we had a problem.

What you're holding is the result of eighteen months of extensive revision.

We have removed, redacted, or replaced the following:

• All references to ■■■■■■■■■■■■■■■■■■
• The complete details of the ■■■■■■■■ operation and its aftermath
• Everything involving the incident in ■■■■■■■■ with the ■■■■■■■■ and the surprisingly aggressive penguins (yes, penguins—no, we will not elaborate)

• Erik's actual interrogation methodology, replaced with a more family-friendly version involving an angle grinder and what we've termed "the practice toe"

• The true nature of what was behind that door (you'll understand when you get there)

• Approximately 847 pages of material that our lawyers described as "literature's most compelling argument for a worldwide amnesia epidemic"

• The parts that made Tootsie pass out (obviously)

The result is what we consider a "G-rated" version of our actual experiences.

By "G-rated," we mean: "will not cause apex predators to lose consciousness."

Your mileage may vary. We recommend reading in a well-ventilated area, with access to emergency services, and perhaps not while operating heavy machinery. Just in case.

A few important notes as you proceed:

1. The names have been changed. Except for ours. We're tired of hiding.

2. The locations have been changed. Except for the ones that haven't. We leave it as an exercise for the reader to determine which is which. (This is not a game. Do not actually try to determine this. Some of those locations are still very much active.)

3. The methods have been simplified. What we actually do is more complicated, more effective, and significantly more disturbing than anything depicted in these pages. This is for your protection. And ours. And Tootsie's.

4. The door is real. We will not elaborate on this point. Ever.

5. Gerald is real. His cat Theodore is also real, and currently judging all of us from his position of supreme feline indifference.

6. The line is real. That's the most important thing to understand. Everything else in this book—the operations, the characters, the jokes about Swiss socks—all of it is in service of that single truth. There is a line. We hold it. That part is not fiction.

If you're reading this foreword and thinking, "Surely they're exaggerating about the tiger," we assure you: we are not.

Tootsie is currently sitting approximately fourteen feet behind us as we write this, watching our keystrokes with the focused intensity of a creature who remembers what that first manuscript did to him. We can confirm that he has not lost consciousness once during the writing of this foreword.

That's how you know it's safe.

That's how you know we've done our job.

If at any point during your reading of this book you feel overwhelmed, disturbed, or in need of a moment to collect yourself, please take comfort in the fact that you are experiencing the *gentle* version. The version specifically calibrated to not overwhelm a 673-pound killing machine. The version we *wanted* to write would have required you to sign forty-seven waivers, undergo a full psychological evaluation, and maintain a minimum safe distance of 200 meters from any populated area.

Consider yourself fortunate.

Now, with all appropriate warnings delivered, we invite you to enter our world.

It's a world of consequences. A world where the line between acceptable and unacceptable is held by people willing to do what others won't. A world that is simultaneously darker and lighter than you might expect—darker because of what people do when they think no one is watching, lighter because sometimes, against all odds, someone *is* watching.

And sometimes, that someone is us.

You're welcome.

— Justin Lampert & Erik Block

P.S. — Tootsie says hello. Unlike Theodore, he actually means it. He has, however, asked us to convey that he would prefer you not show him any future manuscripts. Once was enough. His therapist agrees.

P.P.S. — If you're wondering whether any of this foreword is true: yes. All of it. Especially the parts about the penguins. *Especially* those.

CLASSIFICATION NOTICE

This document has been reviewed, redacted, re-reviewed, re-redacted, partially declassified, immediately re-classified, lost, found, denied, acknowledged, and finally released under protest by no fewer than fourteen agencies across seven countries.

The black bars you will encounter throughout this text are not printing errors. They are load-bearing redactions. Removing them would cause structural collapse of several international agreements and at least one marriage.

If you are reading this without proper clearance, please note that you are now implicated in something you cannot fully understand. This is normal. This is expected. This is, in fact, the safest version of what could have happened to you today.

You're welcome.

PART ONE

The Safe Version

"There is no safe version."

— Ethics Committee Internal Report

"There is always a safe version."

— Justin Lampert, contradicting the above

PROLOGUE

Before They Were Legends

Year One

They met in a room that didn't exist, in a building that had been demolished three years earlier, during a briefing that would never appear in any official record.

Justin Lampert was twenty-eight years old and already tired of being underestimated. He had a law degree he'd never used, a military record that said less than it meant, and a way of looking at people that made them want to confess things they hadn't done yet.

He had been recruited out of JAG Corps after an incident that the official record described as "unauthorized intervention in a local matter" and the unofficial record described as "saving seventeen people by disobeying a direct order." The brass had wanted to court-martial him. Someone higher up had wanted to hire him.

The hiring won.

Erik Block was twenty-eight and had already stopped counting the languages he spoke. He moved through the world like water through cracks—finding the gaps, filling the spaces, disappearing before anyone noticed he'd been there. His file said he was "adaptable." His file was an understatement.

He had no clear origin story—at least not one that anyone could access. Multiple agencies had tried to trace his background. They had all failed. Wherever Erik Block came from, it was a place that didn't leave records.

The man running the briefing was named Collins. He would be dead within the year—not because of anything Erik or Justin did, but because he had a heart condition he'd been ignoring and a job that didn't allow for ignored heart conditions.

"Gentlemen," Collins said, "I'm going to be direct."

Justin glanced at Erik. Erik didn't glance back. He was reading the room—the exits, the sight lines, the quality of the fluorescent lighting that suggested a budget decision made by someone who'd never spent eight hours under it.

"We have a problem," Collins continued. "The problem is that our problems have problems. The world is getting more complicated, and the people we send to uncomplicate it are getting less effective."

He pulled up a slide. It showed a graph that went in a direction graphs weren't supposed to go.

"This is our success rate over the last decade. Notice how it's not going up."

Justin raised his hand. "Is this the part where you tell us we're special?"

Collins came close to smiling. Almost.

"No," he said. "This is the part where I tell you that you're expendable, but in a way that might be useful."

Their first mission together was a disaster.

Not the kind of disaster that made headlines—the quiet kind, the kind that got filed under "lessons learned" and never mentioned again. They were sent to extract a defector from a country that didn't officially have defectors. The defector was supposed to be alone.

He wasn't.

"You didn't mention the family," Justin said, staring at the three children huddled behind their father.

The voice in his earpiece crackled. "The family wasn't in the intelligence."

"The family is in the room," Erik said quietly. It was the first time Justin had heard him speak. "Intelligence doesn't change that."

They had two options. The first was clean, professional, and would leave three orphans. The second was messy, improvised, and would probably get them killed.

Justin looked at Erik.

Erik looked at the children.

"Well," Justin said. "Option two it is."

What followed was later described in the official report as "an unauthorized deviation from operational parameters resulting in unexpectedly positive outcomes." What it actually was: two men, five civilians, and seventeen minutes of the most creative problem-solving either of them had ever done.

They got everyone out.

They got themselves out.

They got a reputation that would follow them for the rest of their careers.

Collins called them into his office three days later.

"You disobeyed direct orders," he said.

"Yes," Justin agreed.

"You endangered the entire operation."

"Also yes."

"You saved five people who weren't part of the mission profile."

"That one's yes too."

Collins leaned back in his chair. He had the look of a man doing math he didn't like.

"Do you know what the problem is with people like you?" Collins asked.

Erik spoke for the first time in the meeting. "We make the statistics look wrong."

Collins stared at him for a long moment.

Then he laughed.

It was not a nice laugh. It was the laugh of a man who had just realized he was holding a tool he didn't know how to use.

"You're going to be trouble," Collins said. "Both of you. You're going to break rules, ignore protocols, and make my life significantly harder."

Justin smiled. "Probably."

Collins nodded slowly.

"Good," he said. "I was worried I'd hired normal people."

Year Two

They developed what would later be called "the Lampert-Block methodology"—though neither of them ever called it that. It wasn't really a methodology. It was more like jazz: you had to know the rules before you could break them, and you had to break them before you could make something new.

The rules they broke were always the same ones.

The rule that said acceptable casualties were acceptable.

The rule that said collateral damage was an unavoidable cost.

The rule that said some people didn't matter because they weren't in the mission profile.

"Why do you care so much?" another operative asked Justin once, after they had saved a family that was supposed to be expendable.

Justin thought about it for a long time.

"Because someone has to," he said finally.

Year Three

People started telling stories.

Some of them were true. The extraction in Minsk where they'd gotten twelve people out of an "impossible" situation. The interrogation in Hamburg where they'd broken a target in eleven minutes without using violence. The rescue in Bogotá where they'd walked into a compound full of armed men and walked out with every hostage alive.

Some of the stories weren't true. The one about the angel wings. The one about the demon contracts. The one about the dead speaking through them.

Justin found the legends amusing.

Erik found them useful.

"Let them believe," Erik said once, when Justin suggested correcting a particularly absurd rumor. "The myths do work we don't have to."

Justin thought about that.

"That's either very cynical or very smart."

"Both," Erik said. "Usually both."

Year Four

Collins died on a Tuesday.

Heart attack. The one he'd been ignoring for years. He collapsed in his office at 3 PM and was dead before anyone could help.

Justin and Erik attended the funeral. Small. Private. The kind of ceremony that happened when the deceased had done work that couldn't be discussed publicly.

Afterward, they sat in a bar that served drinks no one should drink and talked about things no one should discuss.

"He was wrong about us," Justin said.

"Was he?"

"He said we'd be trouble. He didn't say we'd be necessary."

Erik considered this.

"Maybe he did," Erik said. "Maybe that's what 'trouble' meant."

Justin drank his terrible drink.

"You know what I realized today?" he said.

"What?"

"We're going to do this forever. This work. This life. We're going to keep doing it until we can't anymore."

"Yes."

"And it's never going to be enough. No matter how many people we save, how many networks we dismantle, how many lines we hold—it's never going to be enough."

"No," Erik agreed. "It won't."

"So why do we keep doing it?"

Erik considered the question.

"Because someone has to,' he said. It was the same answer Justin had given years earlier. "And because if we stop—if we let the line move, if we decide that some problems aren't our responsibility—then we become part of what we're fighting against."

"That's not an answer."

"No," Erik agreed. "But it's the truth."

Justin thought about that.

"Close enough," he said.

And it was.

Year Five and Beyond

13

They stopped correcting the legends that weren't true.

They let the mythology grow around them like armor, like camouflage, like a weapon in its own right.

And somewhere along the way, without either of them planning it, they became exactly what Collins had predicted: trouble. The useful kind. The kind that solved problems other people couldn't solve because other people were too busy following the rules.

The kind that stood on the line and held it.

Whatever that cost.

Whatever that meant.

Forever.

CHAPTER 1

The Origin

Before the partnership. Before the legend.

Before everything.

Justin Lampert was twenty-three years old when he first crossed the line.

Not the line he would later define, later defend, later build a life around. A smaller line. A personal line. The boundary between the person he had been and the person he was about to become.

It happened in a village in Bosnia that no longer appears on maps.

He was there as a translator. JAG Corps had sent him because he spoke five languages fluently and four others conversationally, and because someone had decided that a village of 847 people needed legal documentation of what had happened to them.

The documentation was extensive.

Seventeen pages of witness statements. Forty-three photographs that would never be published. A list of names—perpetrators, victims, witnesses—that would be filed, classified, and forgotten by everyone except the people who had survived.

Justin read every word. Saw every photograph. Memorized every name.

And then he went back to the base and filed his report and waited for something to happen.

Nothing happened.

"It's not our jurisdiction," his commanding officer explained. "It's a matter for the international courts."

"The international courts have a backlog of seven years."

"Then it's a matter for seven years from now."

"People are dying. The perpetrators are still operating. They're moving to the next village—"

"That's not our concern, Lieutenant."

Justin stared at the man across the desk from him.

"We have names. We have evidence. We have everything needed to—"

"To what?" The commander's voice was tired. The voice of a man who had been having this conversation for twenty years. "To authorize an action that hasn't been approved through proper channels? To take responsibility for consequences that haven't been analyzed by people who get paid to analyze consequences?"

"To do something."

"Something is not in our operational mandate."

Justin stood.

"Then what is?" he asked. "What, exactly, are we here for, if not to do something when we have the ability and the information and the moral obligation?"

The commander didn't answer.

There was no answer.

Or rather, there was an answer, but it wasn't the kind you could say out loud. The answer was: we're here to document. To observe. To create records that will satisfy future historians while doing nothing to help the people whose suffering we're recording.

Justin understood that answer.

He simply couldn't accept it.

He crossed the line three nights later.

Not with authorization. Not with backup. Not with any of the things that military protocol required for operations in hostile territory.

He crossed it alone, in the dark, with a weapon he had taken from the armory and a list of names he had memorized from the file.

The first name was Radovan Mari█.

Mari█ was forty-seven years old. He had commanded the unit responsible for the village. He had personally ordered the deaths of seventeen civilians. He was, according to the official record, "a person of interest" who "may face future prosecution."

He was also sleeping in a farmhouse twelve kilometers from the base, completely unaware that anyone was coming for him.

Justin arrived at 3 AM.

What happened next would later be described in the classified record as "an unauthorized action resulting in the death of a military target."

The classified record was, as usual, incomplete.

What actually happened was this: Justin Lampert kicked in the door of a farmhouse, confronted a man who had murdered seventeen civilians, and gave him a choice.

Surrender. Face justice. Accept accountability.

Or refuse.

Mari█ refused.

He reached for a weapon—there was always a weapon, these men always had weapons—and Justin Lampert discovered something about himself that he had not known before.

He was faster.

He was better.

And when it was over, when Mari█ was dead on the floor of his own farmhouse, Justin felt something he had not expected.

Relief.

Not satisfaction. Not triumph. Not the bloodlust that the movies suggested came with killing.

Just relief.

The simple, quiet relief of knowing that one man—one specific man who had done specific terrible things—would never hurt anyone again.

The investigation took three months.

Justin was questioned extensively. His story was examined from every angle. Experts analyzed the evidence, debated the justifications, considered the implications.

In the end, they reached a conclusion that satisfied no one.

"Unauthorized, but not unjustified."

"A violation of protocol, but not of principle."

"A problem, but not a criminal one."

He was transferred out of JAG Corps. Reassigned to a department that officially didn't exist. Given new handlers, new objectives, new parameters for his particular combination of skills.

And slowly, over the years that followed, he built something.

Not a career. Not a reputation. Something more fundamental.

A purpose.

The second name on his list was Dragan Petrovi■.

He found Petrovi■ two years later, in a café in Belgrade. The man had changed his appearance, moved to a new city, built a new life. He thought he was safe.

He wasn't.

"Do you know who I am?" Justin asked, sitting down across from him.

Petrovi■'s eyes went wide.

"No. No, this isn't—you can't be here—"

"I can be anywhere." Justin's voice was calm. "I can find anyone. And I have a list."

"A list?"

"Names. Seventeen of them. The people you killed in Srebrenica."

Petrovi■'s face went pale.

"That was war. That was—"

"That was murder." Justin leaned forward. "And now you have a choice. The same choice I gave your commander."

"What choice?"

"You can come with me. Face trial. Tell the truth about what happened and who gave the orders."

"And if I refuse?"

Justin smiled.

It was not a pleasant smile.

"Then I stop giving choices."

Petrovi■ came quietly.

Over the next decade, Justin Lampert found every name on his list.

Some came willingly. Some resisted. Some died in circumstances that could never be officially discussed.

But all of them faced consequences.

All of them learned that the line—the boundary they had thought protected them—was not where they believed it was.

And somewhere along the way, Justin stopped being a translator with languages and a conscience. He became something else. Something that the intelligence community didn't have a name for, because they had never seen anything quite like it before.

He became the line itself.

Not a metaphor. Not an abstraction. A living, breathing embodiment of the principle that some things were unacceptable, and that those who did them would be held accountable.

He met Erik Block at the end of that decade.

By then, Justin had a reputation. Stories followed him—some true, some exaggerated, some completely fabricated. He was a ghost. He was a weapon. He was the thing that war criminals whispered about when they thought no one was listening.

Erik had a different reputation.

Erik was silence. Erik was patience. Erik was the ability to wait in shadows for hours, days, weeks, until the perfect moment arrived.

They were introduced by a man named Collins, in a room that didn't exist, during a briefing that would never appear in any official record.

"You're both problems," Collins said. "Too effective to ignore. Too independent to control. The kind of problems that usually solve themselves—either you burn out, or you make a mistake, or someone decides you're more trouble than you're worth."

He looked at them across the table.

"But I have a theory. My theory is that two problems might cancel each other out. That you might balance each other. That together, you might be something more than either of you could be alone."

Justin and Erik looked at each other.

Neither spoke.

But something passed between them. A recognition. An understanding.

A possibility.

"What would you need from us?" Justin asked.

Collins smiled.

"Just one thing. Results."

The results came.

Not immediately. Not easily. But over time, the partnership that Collins had predicted began to take shape.

Justin talked. Erik listened.

Justin planned. Erik executed.

Justin held the line. Erik made sure it didn't move.

And slowly, year by year, operation by operation, they became what they were always meant to be.

Not heroes. Not villains. Not tools of any government or ideology.

Just two men who had decided where the line was.

And committed to holding it.

Whatever the cost.

Forever.

CHAPTER 2

This Is the Safe Version

The angle grinder screamed to life.

That sound alone did half the work.

Justin Lampert leaned against the concrete wall, arms crossed, watching the restrained man's breathing accelerate. Twelve breaths per minute had become twenty-two in the span of three seconds. The body knew what was coming even when the mind refused to accept it.

"You know," Justin said conversationally, "most people at this stage try to negotiate. Offer us something. Money, usually. Sometimes information they think we want but don't actually need."

The man in the chair—Kozlov, according to the file, though files said a lot of things and most of them were lies—said nothing. His jaw was clenched so tight that Justin could hear his teeth grinding from across the room.

"The silent treatment is also popular," Justin continued. "Very stoic. Very professional. It usually lasts about—" He checked his watch, a gesture that was entirely theatrical. "—ninety seconds after Erik starts working."

Erik Block crouched in front of the chair, calm as a man trimming bonsai. He didn't respond to Justin. He rarely did when he was working. There was a stillness to Erik in these moments—a quality of absolute presence that most people found more unsettling than the tools themselves.

The room was unremarkable in the way that rooms designed for this purpose always were. Concrete walls stained with things that cleaning crews had stopped asking about. Concrete floor with a drain in the center—the kind of architectural choice that suggested forethought. Fluorescent lighting that buzzed at a frequency specifically calibrated to induce headaches, installed by someone who understood that discomfort was cumulative.

There was a table in the corner. On the table: the tools.

Most of them were never used. That was the secret that civilians didn't understand about this work. The tools were theater. Props in a play that the subject was writing in their own head, filling in details that were always worse than reality.

The angle grinder, though—the angle grinder was real.

"I'm starting with the toe," Erik said to Kozlov. His voice was conversational. Almost apologetic. The voice of a man explaining that the restaurant was out of the fish special. "Big one. It's sentimental."

He removed Kozlov's boot with the care of a man who had done this before and understood that rushing created problems. The sock came next—gray, expensive, the kind of sock that cost forty dollars and came in packaging that used words like "moisture-wicking" and "antimicrobial."

"Nice socks," Justin observed. "Italian?"

"Swiss," Erik said, not looking up.

"Ah. The Swiss. Good at banking, good at socks, terrible at participating in world events."

Kozlov's foot was pale in the harsh light. Five toes, perfectly normal, about to become four.

"Last chance," Erik said quietly. "The information we need. You know what it is."

Kozlov's eyes darted to Justin. Looking for mercy. Looking for an out. Looking for some indication that this was a bluff, a performance, anything other than what it appeared to be.

Justin shrugged.

"Don't look at me. I'm just here for moral support."

The blade touched skin.

The screaming started immediately.

It was a particular kind of scream—the kind that came from somewhere deeper than the throat. The kind that bypassed conscious thought entirely and emerged from whatever primitive part of the brain still remembered what it meant to be prey.

Blood was everywhere.

This was expected. This was, in fact, precisely calibrated. Erik had a gift for this—knowing exactly how much damage to inflict to create maximum psychological impact with minimum permanent harm. It was a narrow line to walk, and most people couldn't walk it at all.

Erik was wearing a rain parka. Bright yellow. The color of school buses and caution tape. The color of things that wanted to be seen.

Justin was not wearing a rain parka.

"For fuck's sake," Justin said, wiping his face with the sleeve of a jacket that had cost more than the interrogation table. "You said you were easing into it."

"I am." Erik didn't look up from his work. "This is the gentle version."

"The gentle—" Justin gestured at the room, at the blood, at the situation in general. "There's a toe on the floor, Erik."

"It's the practice toe. Everyone gets one."

"That's not a real thing."

"It is now."

Kozlov continued screaming. Then crying. Then—as the initial shock began to fade and the reality of his situation became clear—bargaining.

His English improved dramatically. Funny how that worked. Three hours ago, he had claimed to barely speak the language. Now he was fluent, articulate, and extremely motivated to communicate.

"I tell you! I tell you everything!"

"That's nice," Justin said, moving to crouch in front of him. "But you said that before. Right before you lied to us about the accounts in Cyprus."

"Not lies! Mistakes! Simple mistakes!"

"Mmm." Justin stood and walked to the table, examining the other tools—mostly for show, but Kozlov didn't know that. "The problem with 'simple mistakes' is that they tend to compound. One mistake leads to another. Pretty soon, you've got a whole ecosystem of mistakes, and it becomes hard to trust anything."

He picked up something that looked medical and probably wasn't.

"Erik, what do you think? Has our friend here earned some trust?"

Erik stood, leaving the grinder running on the floor. The sound filled the room—a constant reminder of what could resume at any moment. A promise and a threat in one mechanical whine.

"He's scared," Erik observed. "That's good. But scared people lie. They say whatever they think will make the fear stop."

"True." Justin set down the medical thing and picked up something else. Something with edges. "So how do we know when he's telling the truth?"

"We don't." Erik crouched in front of Kozlov again, meeting his eyes with the calm certainty of a man who had done this a hundred times. "That's his problem, not ours. He has to convince us. And right now—" He glanced at the toe on the floor. "—he hasn't."

Kozlov's face went pale. Paler than the blood loss could account for.

"What you want? Tell me what you want, I give you!"

Justin sighed.

"Okay. Let's try something different."

He walked to the door and knocked once.

Hard.

What happened next is referenced in the official record as:

NON-STANDARD PSYCHOLOGICAL LEVERAGE

>

(SEE ETHICS REVIEW ■■■■-■■ / APPENDIX ■■■■)

The official record is, as usual, incomplete.

What actually happened was this: the door opened, and something was on the other side. Something that Kozlov recognized. Something that made the angle grinder and the blood and the missing toe suddenly seem manageable by comparison.

His eyes locked on it.

His screaming stopped.

That was new. Most people screamed more when they saw it. Kozlov went silent—completely, utterly silent—as if his voice had been surgically removed.

His breathing stopped entirely for three seconds—long enough that Justin briefly wondered if they'd pushed too far, if the combination of physical trauma and psychological shock had been miscalibrated.

Then Kozlov exhaled in a long, shuddering gasp and began to cry in a way that had nothing to do with the pain.

Justin crouched in front of him.

"I want to be clear," he said calmly, almost gently. "Nothing that happens next will be written down correctly. Nothing will be reported accurately. No one will believe you when you tell them what you saw."

He let that sink in.

"So you have a choice. You can tell us what we need to know, right now, completely and truthfully. Or—"

He didn't finish the sentence. He didn't need to.

"Please," Kozlov whispered. "Please, I tell you. Everything. Please just—"

"The accounts," Justin said. "All of them. Not just Cyprus."

"Yes. Yes. Liechtenstein. Singapore. The one in—" He hesitated. Old habits dying hard even in extremis.

"The one in where?" Erik asked quietly.

"Delaware," Kozlov said, and something in him seemed to collapse. "There is one in Delaware. Domestic. No one looks at domestic."

Justin and Erik exchanged a glance.

Delaware. That was new. That wasn't in any of the files.

"Keep talking," Justin said.

Kozlov kept talking.

The subject broke completely.

Information came out fast. Faster than Justin could mentally catalog—not that he was writing anything down, because nothing was being recorded, nothing was being documented, nothing was happening in any official sense.

Names. Kozlov gave them names—handlers, contacts, the entire network he had spent three years protecting. He gave them without hesitation, without the usual attempts to hold back the most valuable pieces as leverage.

Locations. Safe houses in four countries. Server farms. Dead drops. The kind of operational infrastructure that would normally require months of surveillance to map.

Times. Delivery schedules. Meeting protocols. The pattern of rotation that Kozlov's organization used to avoid detection—a pattern that was, as of this moment, completely useless.

Passwords. Account numbers. The digital keys to an empire of secrets.

All of it.

Everything.

In eleven minutes.

When it was over, Kozlov slumped in his chair like a puppet with cut strings. He had given them more than they'd asked for, more than they'd expected, more than they'd dared hope for.

He had given them everything he had.

And in doing so, he had destroyed himself. Burned every bridge. Betrayed every ally. Transformed himself from a valuable asset into a liability that no one would protect.

Justin almost felt sorry for him.

Almost.

"What was it?" Erik asked later, when they were cleaning up.

Justin looked at him. "What was what?"

"Behind the door. What did he see?"

Justin didn't respond immediately.

"You know I can't tell you that."

"Can't or won't?"

"Both." Justin finished wiping down a surface that didn't need wiping. "Some things work better when they're not explained. Some things lose their power when you put them into words."

Erik considered this.

"There's a file," he said. "Somewhere. Documentation of what that thing is. Where it came from."

"There might be."

"Someday I'll read it."

"Someday," Justin agreed. "When the work is done. When we can afford to look at the tools we've been using."

"Is that a promise?"

Justin met his eyes.

"It's an inevitability. Everything comes out eventually. Every mystery gets solved. Every door gets opened." He shrugged. "Just not today."

He thought about the file he kept locked in a place that didn't exist. About the project designation and the clearances required to even know the clearances existed. About why they used it so sparingly—not because it didn't work, but because some tools changed you every time you picked them up.

Erik accepted this with a slight nod.

"That's very philosophical for a man covered in someone else's blood."

"I contain multitudes."

The corner of Erik's mouth twitched.

"The Delaware account," he said, changing the subject. "That's significant."

"Very. Domestic money laundering through a state with corporate secrecy laws. Someone's been clever."

"Someone's been arrogant. They thought we wouldn't look close to home."

Justin nodded. "That's always the mistake. People build these elaborate international networks, shell companies in six countries, accounts scattered across three continents. And then they put the real money somewhere boring. Somewhere no one would think to check."

"Delaware."

"Delaware."

They finished cleaning in silence.

Medical personnel arrived forty-seven minutes later.

They noted—in a report that would be filed, classified, and never read by anyone who mattered—the following observations:

• *Subject displays elevated heart rate (persistent, expected given circumstances)*

• *Partial shock (managed, non-critical)*

• *Blood loss (approximately 400ml, within acceptable parameters)*

• *Digital amputation (right foot, first metatarsal, clean excision)*

• *Psychological state: compliant, cooperative, repeatedly asking "is it gone?"*

• *Note: Subject refuses to specify what "it" refers to*

When asked what had convinced him to cooperate, Kozlov responded:

"He smiled and then
████████████████████████████████████*."*

Clarification was requested.

The request was denied.

Further clarification was requested, more firmly, with references to proper documentation protocols and chain-of-custody requirements.

The request was denied again, with a note suggesting that the requesting party "stop asking questions they don't want answered" and a recommendation to "focus on the intelligence obtained rather than the methods used to obtain it."

The requesting party filed a formal complaint.

The complaint was lost.

INTERNAL MEMORANDUM (UNREQUESTED)

FROM: Ethics Review Committee

>

TO: Everyone Who Will Ignore This

>

RE: Lampert / Block—Yet Again

>

CC: Our Therapists

>

We would like to reiterate, for what we believe is the fourteenth time this fiscal quarter, the following points:

>

1. Improvisation is not a recognized interrogation protocol. When we say "recognized," we mean "approved by any governing body, oversight committee, or rational adult who has passed a background check."

>

2. "We'll figure it out" is not a legal justification for anything. It is certainly not a legal justification for what happened in Room 17. It is not a legal justification for what happened behind the door. It is especially not a legal justification for the thing we're not allowed to ask about.

>

3. The phrase "practice toe" should never appear in official documentation. Or unofficial documentation. Or any documentation. Or conversation. Or thought. We have consulted with three different legal teams and none of them can determine how to classify a "practice toe" under existing regulations.

>

4. Rain parkas are not Personal Protective Equipment within the meaning of any workplace safety regulation. The fact that they are "practical" and "easy to clean" does not change this. The fact that

Agent Block's parka is yellow does not make it a safety device. The fact that it was a gift does not make it sentimental. The fact that we keep bringing this up does not mean we expect anything to change.

>

5. We still do not know what was behind the door. We have been told, repeatedly, that we do not want to know. We are beginning to believe this is accurate.

>

Effective immediately, the committee requests:

>

• *Advance notice of all interrogation activities (minimum 48 hours)*

>

• *Psychological screening of all subjects prior to enhanced questioning*

>

• *At least one witness who doesn't quit afterward*

>

• *A clear explanation of what, exactly, was behind the door*

>

This request will be denied.

>

We know it will be denied.

>

We are filing it anyway, because documentation matters, because the record matters, because someday someone will want to understand how any of this was allowed to happen.

>

And when they ask, we will point to this memo and say: "We tried."

>

That will have to be enough.

>

*ADDENDUM: Agent Lampert has requested that we "lighten up."
Agent Block has not commented. We are choosing to interpret this
silence as agreement with our concerns rather than indifference to
our existence.*

>

*ADDENDUM TO ADDENDUM: We have been informed that our
interpretation is incorrect.*

>

*ADDENDUM TO ADDENDUM TO ADDENDUM: We give up.
Again.*

Outside, the night air felt clean by comparison.

The facility—they never called it by its actual name, because its actual name was classified, and anyway "black site" had such negative connotations—sat on the edge of a city that didn't acknowledge its existence. Three stories of nothing that housed everything. The kind of place that appeared on no maps, answered no questions, and generated approximately four hundred pages of paperwork every time something happened inside it.

Justin stretched his neck, working out the tension that had accumulated during the hours of preparation. The actual work had taken eleven minutes. The preparation had taken three hours. The paperwork would take three days.

This was the job. This was always the job. Brief moments of intensity surrounded by endless tedium.

"The source in Hamburg," Erik said, falling into step beside him as they walked toward their vehicle. "He's going to need relocating."

"Already done. Martinez handled it while we were inside."

"And the account in Liechtenstein?"

"Frozen. The Swiss were actually helpful for once. Something about Kozlov's network threatening their reputation for discretion."

"The Delaware connection?"

"That's tomorrow. Need to be careful with domestic operations. Different rules, different oversight, different ways to get burned."

Erik nodded. Justin could see him processing—cross-referencing the new information against the old, building mental models, identifying the next three steps while they walked.

This was how they worked. Had been working for years. Justin talked; Erik thought. Justin filled silence; Erik made silence useful. Two instruments playing different parts of the same song.

The city sprawled around them—lights and movement and millions of people living their lives, completely unaware of what had happened two miles away in a building that didn't exist.

Justin exhaled slowly.

"You ever think about what they'd say?" he asked. "All those people out there. If they knew what we did."

Erik considered this.

"Some would be grateful," he said finally. "Some would be horrified. Most wouldn't believe it."

"And you? What do you think they should feel?"

Erik considered the question with the seriousness he brought to everything.

"I think feelings are irrelevant," he said. "I think the work matters regardless of how anyone feels about it. I think the line exists whether people acknowledge it or not."

"That's very cold."

"It's very true."

They reached the car. Justin unlocked it with a beep that seemed too mundane for the night they'd had.

"Erik," he said, before they got in.

"Yes?"

"The Delaware thing. It's going to be big. Bigger than Kozlov. Bigger than his whole network."

"I know."

"Are you ready for that?"

Erik half-smiled.

"I'm always ready."

They drove away.

Behind them, the facility sat silent in the darkness, keeping its secrets, holding its horrors, waiting for the next time it would be needed.

There was always a next time.

Somewhere else, in an office that was too small for the importance of the work done inside it, a man named Gerald Morrison opened a report.

He had been reading reports like this for twenty-three years. Had developed systems for processing them—mental filing cabinets, emotional distance, the professional detachment necessary to absorb horror without being destroyed by it.

This report was different.

Not because of the content. Gerald had read worse. Much worse. The kind of things that made the Kozlov interrogation look like a job interview.

It was different because of the pattern it suggested.

He read the report again. Made notes. Cross-referenced with other reports—dozens of them, accumulated over years, each one a puzzle piece in a picture he was only beginning to see.

Lampert and Block.

They were doing something. Building something. Creating a pattern that no one else had noticed because no one else was looking.

Gerald was looking.

And what he saw worried him.

Not because they were dangerous—though they were. Not because they were effective—though they were that too.

What worried him was simpler, and worse.

They were right.

Whatever they were doing, however they were doing it, the results spoke for themselves. Problems solved. Networks dismantled. Lines held.

And Gerald Morrison, who had spent twenty-three years reading reports and writing memos that no one read, was beginning to wonder if maybe—just maybe—he should be helping them instead of documenting them.

It was a dangerous thought.

He wrote it down anyway.

Someone had to keep the record.

CHAPTER 3

Before

The parka was Anna's idea.

"You're going to get blood on everything you own," she said, watching him pack for another trip he couldn't explain. "At least wear something you can throw away."

Erik Block looked at the bright yellow rain jacket she was holding out to him. It was the color of school buses and caution tape and warning signs. The color of things that wanted to be seen, that demanded attention, that refused to be ignored.

"I'm supposed to be invisible," he said.

Anna smiled. She had a way of smiling that made his chest tight—not with pain, but with something worse. Something he didn't have words for. The knowledge, maybe, that he didn't deserve her. That he probably never would. That whatever cosmic accounting had put her in his path had made a clerical error that would eventually be corrected.

"You're never invisible," she said. "You just think you are."

She tossed him the parka.

He caught it.

That was three years, four months, and eleven days ago.

He still remembered the exact count because Erik Block remembered everything. It was a gift and a curse and a professional necessity, and it meant that certain moments—certain looks, certain touches, certain mornings where the light came through the window just right and Anna was still asleep and he could pretend, briefly, that he was someone else—stayed with him forever.

The parka stayed too.

It would stay long after everything else was gone.

They had met in a hospital cafeteria in Frankfurt, which was not where Erik Block expected to meet anyone worth remembering.

He was there because a job had gone sideways. A man in Düsseldorf who was supposed to be alone had turned out to be not alone, and the not-alone part had included a knife, and the knife had found Erik's ribs before Erik had found the man's throat.

Not deep enough to kill. Deep enough to require stitches. Deep enough to generate paperwork that Erik preferred to avoid.

The hospital was a calculated risk. Official medical attention meant official records, but it also meant competent treatment, and the wound was in a location that made self-care impractical. He had weighed the options, made the decision, and now he was sitting in a cafeteria that smelled like industrial coffee and human suffering, waiting for his stitches to be checked and his discharge papers to be processed.

She was sitting three tables away.

He noticed her the way he noticed everything—automatically, professionally, cataloging details without conscious effort. Brown hair, shoulder-length, practical. Clothing that suggested office work, middle-income, nothing flashy. A cup of coffee in front of her that she wasn't drinking.

That last detail caught his attention.

The coffee had been sitting there long enough to develop a skin. Long enough to go cold. Long enough that anyone who actually wanted coffee would have either drunk it or replaced it.

She wasn't there for the coffee.

She was staring at something he couldn't see. Something internal. Something that had pulled her so far inside herself that the external world had ceased to matter.

He recognized that look.

He'd seen it in mirrors.

When she finally noticed him watching—when her eyes refocused on the present and found his—she didn't look away. Didn't flinch. Didn't do any of the things that people usually did when they caught a stranger staring.

"You're bleeding," she said.

Erik looked down. The stitches had torn. Again. A dark stain was spreading through his shirt, the red surprisingly bright against the white fabric.

"It happens," he said.

"You should do something about that."

"Probably."

He didn't move. Neither did she.

The cafeteria hummed around them—the clatter of trays, the murmur of conversations, the ever-present beeping of medical equipment from somewhere nearby. A universe of noise that seemed, somehow, very far away.

"I'm Anna," she said.

"Erik."

"What happened to you, Erik?"

He considered his options. Lies came easily—they always had. He had a dozen cover stories for situations like this, each one practiced until it felt like truth. Industrial accident. Bar fight. Misunderstanding with a door. All the plausible fictions that kept the real world separate from the world he actually lived in.

"I got stabbed," he said.

He wasn't sure why he said it. Maybe because she looked like someone who had already seen enough lies for one day. Maybe because her coffee was cold and she hadn't noticed, and that meant something was breaking inside her, and he didn't want to add to it.

Maybe because he was tired.

She nodded slowly. Taking it in. Processing.

"My father's dying," she said. "Upstairs. Room 412. He doesn't recognize me anymore."

"I'm sorry."

"Are you?"

Erik thought about it. Really thought about it—not the automatic response, not the social lubrication, but the actual truth.

"Yes," he said. "I think I am."

She half-smiled. Just a flicker, there and gone. But he saw it.

"You should get those stitches fixed," she said.

"You should drink your coffee."

"It's cold."

"I know."

She looked at him for a long moment. Something passed between them—not words, not understanding, just recognition.

Two people who were, in their own ways, very far from home.

Then she picked up the cup and drank the cold coffee anyway, grimacing at the taste but finishing it.

"There," she said. "Your turn."

Erik went and got his stitches fixed.

When he came back, she was still there.

He told her what he did for a living on their third date.

Not all of it. Not the details. Not the specific operations, the specific kills, the specific moments where he had become something that most people couldn't imagine.

But enough.

"You hurt people," she said.

They were in her apartment—small, cluttered with books, smelling like the lavender candles she burned to cover the smell of the city. She had a collection of history texts that took up an entire wall, organized not by author or subject but by era—her own personal timeline of human achievement and human failure.

"Yes," he said.

"For money?"

"For reasons. The money is incidental."

"That's worse."

"I know."

She took her time processing this. Erik watched her process it—watched the information move through her, watched her decide how to respond. He had seen this moment before. Had seen it with other women, other attempts at connection, other failures.

Usually this was where they left.

Usually this was where they decided that whatever attraction they felt wasn't worth the weight of what he was.

Anna didn't leave.

"Why are you telling me this?" she asked.

"Because you asked."

"Most people would lie."

"Most people aren't hoping you'll tell them to stop."

The words came out before he could catch them. Before he could filter them through the usual screens, the usual defenses. He hadn't known they were true until he said them.

Anna looked at him. Really looked—not at the surface, not at the carefully constructed exterior, but at something beneath.

"I can't tell you to stop," she said quietly. "That's not my choice to make."

"Whose choice is it?"

"Yours." She reached out and took his hand. Her fingers were warm, surprisingly strong for their size. "It was always yours."

She didn't ask him to stop. She never asked him to change.

What she did was worse.

She made him want to.

Not through ultimatums or tears or the kind of emotional leverage he'd been trained to recognize and resist. Not through manipulation or guilt or any of the tools that people used to control each other.

She simply existed. Fully, completely, without apology.

And that existence—the reality of her, the warmth of her, the way she laughed at terrible jokes and cried at historical documentaries and believed, genuinely believed, that understanding the past could prevent its repetition—that existence revealed everything that was hollow in his own.

She taught middle school. History. She cared about it in a way that he had never seen anyone care about anything—not performatively, not professionally, but genuinely. When she talked about the Weimar Republic or the fall of Rome or the thousand small decisions that turned civilizations into dust, her eyes lit up with a conviction that Erik envied without understanding.

She believed in things.

He had stopped believing in things a long time ago.

"You think you're too broken for this," she told him once.

They were lying in bed. The room was dark except for the streetlight outside, and she was tracing the scars on his chest with her fingertips—reading them like a map of everywhere he'd been and everything he'd survived.

"For me," she continued. "For any of this. You think the things you've done have damaged you beyond repair."

"They have."

"No." She kissed the worst scar—the one from Minsk, the one that had nearly killed him, the one that still ached when the weather changed. "You're just trained to believe that broken things should be thrown away."

"Shouldn't they?"

"Nothing is broken beyond repair," she said. "Some things just take longer."

He wanted to believe her.

For eighteen months, he almost did.

The job in Prague was supposed to be simple.

They were all supposed to be simple.

A data center. A server farm containing information that powerful people wanted destroyed. Erik was there to ensure the destruction happened and that no one who shouldn't survive did.

Standard operation. Standard parameters. Standard risk assessment.

He brought the yellow parka because Anna had packed it in his bag without telling him. He found it when he was getting dressed for the job, tucked between his equipment, and he had smiled despite himself.

She worried about him getting blood on his clothes.

He loved her for that.

The job went sideways at 3:17 AM.

The building was supposed to be empty except for guards—three of them, according to the intelligence, rotating on a predictable schedule. Erik's team had planned for the guards. Had planned for every contingency that the intelligence suggested.

The intelligence was wrong.

There were seventeen other people in the building. Analysts working late. Technicians running maintenance. A cleaning crew that wasn't on any manifest because they had been hired through a subcontractor that the intelligence hadn't identified.

Civilians.

Erik's team didn't hesitate. They had orders. They had training. They had the kind of mission-focused discipline that didn't ask questions about collateral damage.

Erik hesitated.

Just for a moment. Just long enough to see them—the analysts with their coffee cups, the technicians with their headphones, the woman with the mop bucket who was humming something he almost recognized.

Civilians.

He made a decision.

He broke protocol. He warned them. He gave them a chance to run, to escape, to survive the operation they weren't supposed to know was happening.

Most of them took it.

For thirty seconds, he thought he'd threaded the needle. Thought he'd found a way to complete the mission without adding seventeen names to the list he carried.

Then the shooting started.

When it was over, the building was burning and Erik was standing in the snow outside, watching fire trucks that wouldn't arrive in time.

The yellow parka was splattered with blood that wasn't his.

He couldn't feel his hands.

Fourteen people made it out.

Three didn't.

Including the woman with the mop bucket, who had gone back for her phone. Her name, he would learn later, was Marta. She was fifty-seven years old. She had two grandchildren.

She had been humming a song by Edith Piaf.

He learned all of this from a file he shouldn't have accessed, because he needed to know. Because not knowing felt like another kind of murder.

Because her face wouldn't leave him, and he thought that if he could just understand who she was—who she had been—it might somehow make the weight of her death easier to carry.

It didn't.

It never did.

Anna knew something was wrong the moment she saw him.

He walked through the door of her apartment and she looked up from the papers she was grading and her face changed. Not dramatically. Just a slight shift—a tightening around the eyes, a tension in her shoulders.

She knew.

"What happened?" she asked.

He told her.

All of it. The job. The civilians. The choice he'd made and the choice that hadn't mattered. Marta and her phone and the fire that had taken her.

Everything.

Anna listened. She didn't interrupt. She didn't comfort. She didn't try to make him feel better with platitudes about doing his best or circumstances beyond his control.

When he was done, when the words ran out and there was nothing left but silence and the weight of what he'd admitted, she said:

"And you think this means you should stop."

"Shouldn't I?"

She didn't answer right away. The apartment was very still. Outside, the city continued—traffic and sirens and the endless noise of people living their lives—but inside, there was only this.

"If you stopped," she said finally, "who would warn the next seventeen people?"

He didn't have an answer.

"You're not a monster," she said. "Monsters don't feel this. Monsters don't come home and confess. Monsters don't lie awake wondering about the grandchildren of a woman they couldn't save."

She moved closer to him. Took his face in her hands. Made him look at her.

"You're just a person," she said. "Doing impossible things and being crushed by the weight of them. That's not evil. That's human."

"That's not better."

"No," she agreed. "But it's survivable."

She held him that night. Held him while he didn't cry because he'd trained himself not to. Held him while his body shook with something that wanted to be grief but didn't know how.

"I love you," she whispered. "Even the broken parts. Especially the broken parts."

He believed her.

That was his mistake.

They came for him two months later.

Not for him, precisely.

For Anna.

She was the leverage. The pressure point. The vulnerability he hadn't known he had until someone exploited it.

He came home from a job—a short one, simple, the kind of operation that didn't usually stay with him—and the apartment was wrong.

The silence was wrong.

The smell of lavender was there, but underneath it was something else. Something copper and final.

He found her in the bedroom.

She was still alive when he reached her.

That was the cruelty of it. They hadn't killed her—they'd left her dying. Because dying took time, and time was a message, and the message was: *we can reach you anywhere, we can touch anything you love, and there is nothing you can do to stop us.*

"Erik," she whispered.

He held her. Forgot his training, forgot his discipline, forgot everything except the weight of her in his arms and the blood soaking through the yellow parka he was still wearing.

"I'm here," he said. "I'm here. You're going to be okay."

She smiled. That smile. The one that made his chest tight.

"You're a terrible liar," she said.

"Anna—"

"It's okay." Her voice was fading, each word costing more than the last. "It's not your fault."

"It is."

"It isn't." She reached up, touched his face with fingers that were already cold. "You warned seventeen people. Remember that. When it gets dark—remember that."

"I can't—"

"You can." Her eyes were drifting closed. "You have to. Promise me."

"Anna—"

"Promise me."

He promised.

She died eleven minutes later, in his arms, in the bedroom of an apartment that smelled like lavender and copper, while he wore the yellow parka she had given him because she worried about him getting blood on his clothes.

He found them, eventually.

The men who had killed her. The organization that had ordered it. The chain of command that had decided Anna Richter, middle school history teacher, was an acceptable cost.

He found them.

And then—

The Ethics Committee file on that week runs 847 pages.

Most of it is redacted.

The parts that aren't include the phrase "disproportionate response" eleven times. The phrase "we recommend never discussing this again" appears twice. And there is one sentence that someone forgot to black out:

He made them watch.

When it was over, Erik Block stood in a room that used to contain people who had thought they were untouchable, and he understood something he hadn't understood before.

He wasn't going to stop.

He couldn't stop.

But he could choose. He could decide who he hurt and why. He could make sure that the people who deserved it were the ones who received it.

That was the line.

That was his line.

He kept the parka.

He never washed it.

Justin Lampert found him three months later.

Erik was in a bar in Lisbon, drinking whiskey he didn't taste, watching the door like he always watched doors now.

Justin sat down next to him.

"You're Erik Block," Justin said. "You killed fourteen people in Hamburg last month."

"Did I."

"The official story is that they killed each other. Some kind of internal dispute." Justin smiled. "Nobody believes the official story."

Erik turned to look at him. Really look.

Justin was tall, well-dressed, radiating a confidence that came from either genuine competence or genuine sociopathy. Probably both.

"What do you want?" Erik asked.

"I want to offer you a job."

"I have a job."

"No," Justin said. "You have a crusade. That's different."

Erik's hand moved toward the knife in his boot.

"If I wanted you dead," Justin said calmly, "I wouldn't have sat down next to you. I would have had someone through the kitchen, someone through the bathroom window, and someone through the front door. Simultaneously."

"You've been watching me."

"For two weeks."

"Then you know I don't work with people."

"You did once."

Erik's hand stopped.

"That was different."

"Was it?"

Silence.

Justin reached into his pocket and pulled out a photograph. He slid it across the bar.

A man in a suit. Silver hair. The kind of face that appeared in financial magazines.

"His name is Heinrich Müller," Justin said. "He launders money for people who traffic children. He's been doing it for thirty years. He is very, very careful, and he is very, very protected."

Erik studied the photo.

"Why do you care?"

"Because someone should." Justin's voice was different now. Less polished. "Because the line where responsibility stops keeps moving back, and no one's willing to hold it."

He tapped the photograph.

"Müller is on the wrong side. So are the people who protect him. I want to do something about that."

"And you need me."

"I need someone who understands that some things can't be fixed with paperwork. Someone who knows what it costs and does it anyway."

The silence stretched between them.

He thought about Anna.

About Marta.

About the seventeen people he'd warned.

"Room 714," he said. "Across the street. Twenty minutes."

He stood.

"Erik," Justin said.

Erik paused.

"I'm sorry. About Anna. I read the file."

Erik didn't respond. Didn't acknowledge. Just walked out into the Lisbon night, toward a meeting that would change everything.

The parka is yellow.

The blood washes out if you're careful, but Erik is rarely careful anymore. The stains have accumulated into something like a pattern. Something like a history. Something that tells a story only he can read.

He wears it anyway.

He wears it because it reminds him of what he's lost.

He wears it because it reminds him of why he keeps going.

He wears it because somewhere, in a hospital cafeteria in Frankfurt, a woman with sad eyes and cold coffee looked at him and saw something worth saving.

She was wrong, probably.

But he's going to keep trying to deserve it anyway.

That's the line.

That's his line.

And it holds.

CHAPTER 4

The Partnership

They had been working together for six years before Erik told Justin about Anna.

Not because he was hiding it. Not because it was a secret. But because Erik Block did not talk about things that hurt, and Anna was the thing that hurt most.

It happened in a safe house in Ljubljana, after an operation that had gone sideways in ways that neither of them had anticipated. Three hours of improvisation. Two near-misses. One moment where Erik had been certain—absolutely certain—that they were both going to die.

They hadn't died.

But the certainty lingered.

"You should know," Erik said, breaking a silence that had lasted forty-five minutes.

Justin looked up from the equipment he was cleaning. They always cleaned equipment after operations. It was meditative. It was necessary. It was something to do with hands that wanted to shake.

"Know what?"

"There was someone. Before."

Justin set down the cloth he was holding.

"Okay."

"Her name was Anna."

And then Erik talked.

He talked for three hours. He told Justin about the hospital cafeteria and the cold coffee. About the yellow parka and the gentle teasing. About the eighteen months when he had been almost happy, almost human, almost free of the weight that he carried everywhere.

About the day he came home and found her dying.

About what he did afterward.

About the men who had thought they could hurt him through her, and what it had cost them to learn otherwise.

Justin listened.

He didn't interrupt. Didn't comfort. Didn't offer platitudes or sympathy. He just listened, because listening was what Erik needed, and because Justin understood that some things could only be shared, not fixed.

When Erik finished, the sun was coming up. Golden light spilled through the windows of the safe house, illuminating a room that had witnessed more confessions than any church.

"The parka," Justin said finally.

"What about it?"

"You still wear it."

Erik was quiet.

"She gave it to me because she worried about the blood."

"I know."

"I wear it because—" Erik stopped. Started again. "I wear it because it reminds me. Of her. Of what I lost. Of why I keep doing this."

Justin nodded slowly.

"We all have something," he said. "Something that keeps us going when everything else says we should stop."

"What's yours?"

Justin thought about the question.

"A decision," he said finally. "A long time ago. A moment when I could have walked away, could have let someone else handle it, could have told myself it wasn't my responsibility."

"What happened?"

"I didn't walk away." Justin smiled, but there was no humor in it. "And seventeen people lived who would have died. And I realized that the line—the place where responsibility stops—isn't something that exists outside of us. It's something we choose. Something we create. Something we carry."

Erik considered this.

"So we're both running from something," he said.

"Or toward something. Depends on how you look at it."

49

"Does it matter?"

Justin stood and walked to the window. The sun was higher now. The city was waking up. Somewhere out there, people were starting their days, going to work, living lives that had no idea what had happened in a safe house nearby.

"It matters that we keep going," Justin said. "It matters that we don't stop. It matters that when we see the line—when we see someone crossing it—we do something about it."

He turned.

"That's what this partnership is, Erik. Not friendship. Not convenience. It's two people who have decided where the line is and committed to holding it. Together."

Erik considered the question.

"Together," he agreed.

And that was enough.

The partnership changed after Ljubljana.

Not dramatically. Not in ways that outside observers would notice. But between them, something had shifted.

They started talking more. Not about operations—they had always talked about operations. But about other things. Books. Music. The small observations that make up a life.

Justin learned that Erik had once wanted to be an architect. That he could name every bone in the human body in four languages. That he had a sister he hadn't spoken to in fifteen years, and that he thought about her every day.

Erik learned that Justin had grown up in a small town in Nebraska. That his father had been a minister who lost his faith and his mother had been a teacher who never lost her patience. That Justin had memorized poetry as a child and still recited it when he couldn't sleep.

They learned each other.

And in learning each other, they became something more than partners. More than colleagues. More than two men who did terrible things for necessary reasons.

They became friends.

"Do you ever think about stopping?" Erik asked once, years later.

They were in a hotel room in Tokyo, recovering from an operation that had gone well but felt wrong. Sometimes operations felt wrong even when they succeeded. Sometimes holding the line meant doing things that left marks.

"All the time," Justin admitted.

"But you don't stop."

"Neither do you."

Erik was quiet.

"I used to think I kept going for Anna," he said. "To honor her memory. To make sure her death meant something."

"And now?"

"Now I think I keep going because I don't know how to do anything else." He looked at Justin. "This is who I am. Not who I was before, not who I might have been. Just... this."

Justin nodded.

"When I was twenty-two," he said, "I had a plan. Law school, maybe politics. A normal life with normal problems. I was going to be somebody important."

"And?"

"And then I saw what important people were willing to ignore. The compromises they made. The lines they let move because moving the line was easier than holding it."

He stood and walked to the window.

"I decided I didn't want to be important. I wanted to be useful."

"Is that what this is? Being useful?"

"It's what I can do. It's what I'm good at. And it's necessary—genuinely, actually necessary—in a way that most things aren't."

Erik considered this.

"Anna would have liked you," he said.

It was the first time he had said her name in years.

Justin turned from the window.

"I would have liked her," he said. "Anyone who could put up with you must have been remarkable."

51

Something flickered in Erik's eyes.

"She was."

They sat in silence, two men who had found each other in a world that tried to keep people apart.

Not friends in any conventional sense.

Something deeper.

Something that didn't have a name because names were too small for what it was.

Partners.

Brothers.

The only people in the world who understood what it cost to hold the line, and why it mattered to pay that cost anyway.

ETHICS COMMITTEE—PSYCHOLOGICAL PROFILE UPDATE

SUBJECT: Lampert, Justin / Block, Erik—Partnership Analysis

STATUS: Ongoing

The Committee has attempted to analyze the Lampert/Block partnership using standard frameworks for professional collaboration.

All frameworks have failed.

Observations:

1. The subjects demonstrate a level of coordination that exceeds any documented partnership in our records

>

2. Communication between subjects frequently occurs through non-verbal means that cannot be analyzed or replicated

>

3. Decision-making appears to be shared, but the mechanism of that sharing remains unclear

>

4. Neither subject has shown any inclination to operate independently, despite opportunities to do so

Assessment:

The partnership is not based on mutual benefit, shared goals, or strategic alignment. These factors are present, but they do not explain the depth of the connection.

The partnership appears to be based on something more fundamental: shared conviction. Both subjects believe in the same principles, hold the same lines, and have committed to the same work.

This makes them extremely effective.

It also makes them extremely dangerous.

Recommendation:

Do not attempt to separate them. Previous attempts to isolate individual assets have failed catastrophically. The partnership is the asset. Treat it accordingly.

Note: We have no idea how to "treat it accordingly." We are simply placing this recommendation on record so that when things inevitably go wrong, we can point to it and say we tried.

CHAPTER 5

The People Who Try

The briefing room smelled like burnt coffee and desperation.

Marcus Vale had been pacing for twenty minutes. Back and forth, back and forth, his footsteps marking a path in the industrial carpet that suggested he'd been doing this for a while. Days, maybe. Weeks.

Caleb Rook sat perfectly still at the table, hands folded, watching the paused image on the screen. He had the posture of a man who believed in preparation—in plans, in discipline, in the kind of careful methodology that separated professionals from amateurs.

Vale was the other kind.

"So let me get this straight," Vale said, stopping mid-pace to gesture at the frozen footage. "Two guys. No backup. No official sanction. No bureaucratic oversight. And they just—"

"They just," Rook confirmed.

The footage showed the aftermath of something that shouldn't have been possible. A warehouse that had contained fourteen members of the Koralev organization—experienced operators, well-armed, thoroughly paranoid—and now contained only problems.

Bodies in positions that suggested they had been neutralized with surgical precision. No wasted movement. No collateral damage. No evidence of the chaos that typically accompanied this kind of work.

Just efficiency.

Terrible, beautiful efficiency.

"We could do that," Vale said. His eyes were bright with something that Rook didn't like. Something hungry.

"No." Rook's voice was flat. "We couldn't."

"Why not? Two guys, right? It's not magic."

"No. It's worse."

Vale scoffed. Resumed his pacing.

Rook studied the screen.

He had been analyzing Lampert and Block for three weeks now, ever since their names had surfaced in connection with the Koralev situation. Not their methods—those were obvious enough. Anyone with training could recognize violence. What Rook studied was the negative space.

The moments when nothing happened.

The pauses. The silences. The fact that, somehow, the outcome always felt decided before anyone moved.

"They don't rely on fear," Rook said finally.

Vale snorted. "Look at that room. That's pure fear."

"No," Rook replied. "Fear is the exhaust. The engine is something else."

"Engine." Vale cracked his knuckles—a habit that Rook found irritating and revealing in equal measure. "Right. Well, I've got an engine too."

He turned to face Rook directly.

"I've got skills. Training. Resources. Everything they have, I can match."

"Can you?"

"What's that supposed to mean?"

Rook considered his response carefully. Vale was volatile—useful in certain contexts, dangerous in others. The wrong word could set him off, and a set-off Vale was an unpredictable Vale.

"They've been doing this for years," Rook said. "Building a reputation. Establishing networks. Learning which lines can be crossed and which ones can't."

"Lines are for people who are afraid to cross them."

"Lines are for people who understand consequences."

Silence.

Vale's jaw tightened.

"You know what I think?" Vale said. "I think you're scared. I think you look at what they've accomplished and instead of seeing opportunity, you see limits. That's why you'll never be more than a watcher, Caleb. That's why you'll spend your whole career sitting in rooms like this, analyzing people who actually do things."

Rook didn't respond.

He was thinking about the footage. About the pattern he'd identified—the subtle tells that suggested not just skill but principle. Lampert and Block weren't random. They were selective. They chose their targets carefully.

They had rules.

And Vale, for all his ambition, had never understood rules.

ETHICS COMMITTEE—INTERNAL MEMORANDUM

FROM: Office of Professional Standards

>

TO: All Personnel

>

SUBJECT: Unauthorized Replication Attempts

>

STATUS: Increasingly Concerning

>

It has come to our attention that certain parties outside the Lampert/Block operational sphere are attempting to "replicate" their methodology.

>

We wish to emphasize the following points:

>

1. There is no methodology. There is only outcome.

>

2. The outcome is achieved through means that cannot be documented, trained, or reproduced by normal operational standards.

>

3. Previous replication attempts have resulted in:

- Three hospitalizations (one critical)

- One international incident requiring diplomatic intervention

- An email chain that caused two senior analysts to request immediate stress leave

- Property damage estimated at $2.4 million

- A congressional inquiry that was, fortunately, terminated before it could produce findings

>

4. Please stop trying.

>

This memorandum constitutes official notice that whatever you're planning, don't.

>

ADDENDUM: We have been informed that this memorandum will be ignored. We are placing it on record anyway, so that when the inevitable inquiry occurs, we can point to it and say "we warned you." This is not petty. This is protocol.

The warehouse smelled like oil and rust and the particular kind of fear that came from knowing things had already gone wrong.

Marcus Vale stood over the man in the chair, breathing hard. His sleeves were rolled up. His smile was too wide.

"See?" Vale said to no one in particular. "That's how it's done."

The man in the chair wasn't talking.

He was screaming.

Rook watched from behind the one-way glass, arms crossed, jaw tight. This wasn't an interrogation. This was performance. Vale wanted the man to break, yes—wanted the information he claimed to need—but he wanted an audience more.

He wanted someone to see him being powerful.

"He's rushing," Rook said into the radio. "The subject isn't ready. He's just making noise."

Vale didn't respond. Couldn't hear anything over the sounds he was making.

Through the glass, Rook watched the scene deteriorate. Vale was escalating—moving faster, pushing harder, losing whatever slim grasp on methodology he'd started with.

The man in the chair was named Petrov. A courier. Low-level. Probably didn't know anything useful, but Vale had convinced himself otherwise.

Vale had convinced himself of a lot of things.

Ten minutes later, Petrov passed out from shock.

No information.

Just noise. Just pain. Just a man in a chair who had been broken for no purpose.

Vale turned to the glass, face splattered with something that wasn't his, still smiling.

"Tough one," he said. "We'll try again when he wakes up."

Rook didn't respond.

He was already writing the report in his head. Already calculating how far this would fall before someone official noticed. Already wondering if he could distance himself from Vale before the inevitable reckoning.

Already knowing that he couldn't.

The answer came three days later.

Vale had found a new subject. Better intelligence this time, he claimed. Someone who definitely knew something worth knowing.

The someone turned out to be wrong.

Wrong name. Wrong affiliation. Wrong everything.

The intelligence had been fabricated—fed through channels that Vale had never bothered to verify, by sources that had their own reasons for pointing him in the wrong direction.

By the time Rook reached the room, it was too late.

The man on the floor wasn't moving.

Vale stood over him, tools still in hand, wearing an expression that couldn't decide between horror and defiance.

"He shouldn't have—" Vale started.

"Shouldn't have what?" Rook's voice was ice. "Shouldn't have been innocent?"

"The intel said—"

"The intel was wrong. And now a man is dead because you wanted to play at being something you're not."

Vale's face hardened.

"I am what I need to be."

"No." Rook looked at the body. At the blood. At the mess that would take more than mops to clean up. "You're a liability. You've been a liability since day one. The only reason I stayed was because I thought I could moderate you."

He met Vale's eyes.

"I was wrong."

He turned to leave.

"Where are you going?" Vale demanded.

"Away. Before this becomes my problem too."

"It's already your problem. You were here. You watched."

Rook stopped at the door.

"I watched you fail," he said quietly. "And I watched an innocent man die because of it. That's going to stay with me for a long time."

He looked back at Vale.

"But you? You're going to keep doing this. You're going to keep escalating. And eventually, someone is going to notice."

"Who?" Vale's voice was contemptuous. "The Ethics Committee? They don't do anything."

"No. Not the committee."

Rook opened the door.

"Lampert and Block," he said. "They pay attention to people like you."

Vale's smile faltered.

"They don't—"

"They do. They have patterns. Behaviors they watch for. Lines they've drawn. And you, Marcus—you've been crossing every single one."

Rook walked out.

Behind him, Vale stood alone in a room with a body and a future that had just gotten significantly shorter.

Justin Lampert learned about Marcus Vale on a Tuesday.

He was eating lunch at a café in Vienna—a city he happened to be passing through on his way to somewhere else—when his phone buzzed with a message from someone who didn't officially exist.

The message was simple:

New player. Concerning patterns. File attached.

Justin opened the file while finishing his schnitzel.

By the time he reached the dessert menu, he understood the concern.

"Erik," he said into the phone. "We have a problem."

Erik's voice was calm on the other end. It was always calm. "Another one?"

"The special kind. Someone's playing dress-up."

A pause.

"Where?"

"Eastern seaboard. Started about three weeks ago. Multiple interrogations that went wrong. At least one body—maybe more."

"Innocent?"

"Wrong place, wrong time. Mistaken identity."

Another pause, longer this time.

"That's not dress-up," Erik said finally. "That's murder."

"I know." Justin signaled for the check. "The question is whether we intervene now or let it burn itself out."

"If we let it burn, more innocents die."

"If we intervene, we validate. Every wannabe with a grudge will think they can get our attention by escalating."

Silence on the line.

Then Erik said: "There's a line."

"I know."

"And they crossed it."

"I know."

"So we don't have a choice."

Justin sighed. He'd known this would be the answer. Had known it before he made the call.

"No," he agreed. "We don't."

The meeting happened in a parking garage in Baltimore.

Not because parking garages were particularly dramatic—they weren't, really—but because they had concrete floors that were easy to clean, poor lighting that made identification difficult, and enough acoustic dampness that conversations stayed private.

Vale arrived first. Confident. Armed. Alone.

Erik arrived second. Silent. Watchful. Not alone, though Vale didn't know that yet.

"Marcus Vale," Erik said.

Vale turned. His hand moved toward his weapon—an instinctive response that revealed more than he probably intended.

"I wouldn't," Erik said. His voice was conversational. Almost friendly. "You have a gun. I have three minutes of footage showing you killing an innocent man. One of us is protected by documentation. The other isn't."

Vale's hand stopped.

"Who the fuck are you?"

"Someone who pays attention." Erik stepped forward, into the pool of light from the garage's single functioning bulb. The yellow parka seemed to glow in the dim space. "You've been playing a game. Pretending to be something you're not. Hurting people who don't deserve it."

"I don't know what—"

"You know exactly what I'm talking about." Erik's voice didn't rise. It didn't need to. "The man in the warehouse. The one you killed because your intelligence was fabricated. His name was Anton Petrov. He was a janitor. He had three children."

Vale's face went pale.

"How do you—"

"Because I make it my business to know. Because there are people in this world who do what you think you do, but we do it for reasons. With discipline. With rules."

He stepped closer.

"You wanted to be us," he said quietly. "You watched the footage. Studied the methods. Thought you could replicate the outcome without understanding the process."

"I was—"

"You were playing." Erik's eyes were cold. Not angry—just cold. The cold of deep water. "And Anton Petrov paid for your game with his life."

Silence in the garage. Just the distant sound of traffic and the hum of the building's ventilation system.

"So here's what happens now," Erik continued. "You stop. You walk away from this—from all of this. You find another hobby. Something that doesn't involve hurting people."

"And if I don't?"

Erik smiled.

It was not a reassuring smile.

"Then I stop pretending this is a conversation," he said, "and I start treating it like an intervention."

Vale stared at him.

For a moment—just a moment—something like defiance flickered in his eyes. The remnants of the confidence that had brought him here, that had convinced him he was destined for greatness.

Then it died.

"Fine," Vale said. His voice was smaller now. Defeated. "I'm done."

"Good." Erik turned to leave. "One more thing."

"What?"

"Caleb Rook. Your former partner. He was smart enough to walk away. You should thank him."

Vale frowned. "Why?"

"Because he's the reason you're still breathing," Erik said. "He called us. He gave us everything. He's the reason this is a warning instead of a resolution."

Erik disappeared into the darkness of the garage.

Behind him, Marcus Vale stood alone, trembling, finally understanding what it meant to play at being something he wasn't.

Caleb Rook received a text message three hours later.

It said: *Handled. He won't trouble you. We're watching.*

There was no signature. No number he recognized. No way to respond.

But he knew who it was from.

He deleted the message and went back to his life—a life that would, from that moment on, be considerably quieter.

Years later, he would tell the story to people who asked about the scars on his hands—the ones he'd gotten in that warehouse, trying to hold Vale back from a man who was already dying.

He would leave out the names.

He would leave out the worst parts.

But he would always mention the lesson.

"There are people in this world," he would say, "who do things that can't be explained. Things that shouldn't be possible. And the only thing worse than being their enemy is being their disappointment."

People usually laughed when he said this.

Rook never did.

He knew better.

CHAPTER 6

The Delaware Trail

The state of Delaware had two claims to fame.

The first was being the first state to ratify the Constitution, a historical footnote that appeared in textbooks and then promptly disappeared from memory.

The second was corporate law—specifically, the kind of corporate law that allowed people to create companies without revealing who owned them. More than a million businesses were registered in Delaware, most of them existing only on paper, most of them designed to hide money that didn't want to be found.

Justin Lampert had always found this amusing. The United States lectured other countries about financial transparency while hosting the world's most efficient secrecy jurisdiction in a state roughly the size of a shopping mall.

"It's not even a real place," he said, staring out the window of their rental car at the Wilmington skyline. "It's a legal fiction that happens to have geography."

Erik Block was driving. Erik usually drove. He found it meditative—the focus required to navigate traffic while simultaneously processing whatever operational concerns occupied his mind.

"The building is real," Erik said. "1209 North Orange Street. Registered address for over 285,000 companies."

"I know. I've read the articles." Justin pulled up his phone. "One building. 285,000 companies. And somewhere in that mess is the account Kozlov mentioned."

"Ridgewater Holdings LLC."

"Registered six years ago. No employees. No physical presence. Just a name on a piece of paper that moves money from places it shouldn't be to places no one looks."

Erik pulled into a parking garage three blocks from their destination.

"The approach?" he asked.

"Direct. We're not here to investigate. We're here to apply pressure."

"To whom?"

Justin smiled. It was not a pleasant smile.

"Everyone."

The law firm of Hartwell, Chen & Associates occupied the top floor of a building that screamed respectability. Marble floors. Tasteful art. The kind of quiet that came from expensive soundproofing and the absence of anything as vulgar as actual legal work.

The receptionist looked up as Justin and Erik entered.

"Good morning. Do you have an appointment?"

"We do not," Justin said pleasantly. "But we'd like to speak with someone about Ridgewater Holdings."

The receptionist's expression didn't change, but something behind her eyes shifted. A micro-reaction that lasted less than a second and revealed everything.

"I'm sorry, I'm not familiar with that name. Perhaps if you could—"

"Let me rephrase." Justin leaned on the reception desk, still smiling. "We're here about Ridgewater Holdings. The Delaware LLC that your firm registered six years ago. The one that's been moving money for people who would prefer that money not be traced."

The receptionist reached for her phone.

"I'm going to have to ask you to leave."

"That's fine. We'll leave. But first, we're going to speak with Martin Chen. Tell him it's about the Kozlov network. Tell him we have documentation. Tell him—" Justin's smile widened. "—tell him the line has been crossed, and we're here to discuss the consequences."

The receptionist stared at him.

Then she picked up the phone.

Martin Chen was exactly what Justin had expected: mid-fifties, expensive suit, a face that had spent decades learning how to reveal nothing. He met them in a conference room with windows that overlooked the city and furniture that cost more than most people's cars.

"Gentlemen," Chen said, not offering his hand. "I'm told you're making accusations about one of our clients."

"Not accusations," Justin replied. "Statements of fact. Ridgewater Holdings has processed approximately forty-seven million dollars in the past three years. The money originated from accounts linked to human trafficking operations in Eastern Europe. It was cleaned through a series of shell companies and emerged as legitimate investment capital."

He sat down without being invited.

"You knew this. Your firm facilitated it. And now we're going to discuss what happens next."

Chen's expression remained professionally neutral.

"I'm not sure who you think you are, but these kinds of accusations require—"

"Evidence?" Justin pulled a folder from his jacket and slid it across the table. "Transaction records. Account numbers. Email correspondence between your firm and representatives of the Kozlov network. It's all there. Feel free to review it."

Chen didn't touch the folder.

"Even if any of this were accurate—which I'm not conceding—what exactly do you expect to accomplish?"

"I expect you to cooperate."

"Cooperate how?"

Justin looked at Erik. Erik, who had been standing by the door, silent as always, moved to the window and looked out at the city.

"The money trail," Justin said. "Ridgewater is just one node in a larger network. We need to know where the money went after it left your hands. Names. Accounts. Destinations."

"And if I refuse?"

"Then this folder goes to the FBI. The SEC. The Delaware Attorney General. Every journalist who's ever written about corporate secrecy and shell companies." Justin shrugged. "Your firm will be destroyed. Your personal assets will be frozen. Your clients—the ones who trusted you to keep their secrets—will learn that their trust was misplaced."

Chen didn't respond immediately.

"You're not law enforcement," he said finally.

"No."

"You're not government."

"Also no."

"Then what are you?"

Justin smiled.

"We're the people who clean up the messes that law enforcement can't reach. We're the consequence that arrives when the system fails. We're—" He paused, considering his words. "We're the line."

"The line?"

"The line where responsibility stops. The boundary that separates acceptable from unacceptable. You crossed it, Mr. Chen. You helped people move money that was earned by selling human beings. And now you're going to help us stop them."

Chen stared at him.

For a moment—just a moment—something like fear flickered in his eyes. The fear of a man who had spent his career believing he was protected, suddenly realizing that protection had limits.

"What guarantees do I have?" Chen asked quietly.

"None," Justin admitted. "But here's what I can tell you: if you cooperate, fully and completely, we'll focus our attention elsewhere. Your firm will survive. You'll have to live with what you've done, but you'll be alive to live with it."

"And if I don't cooperate?"

Erik turned from the window.

"Then we become creative," he said. It was the first time he'd spoken since they entered the building. "And creativity, in our line of work, tends to be unpleasant for everyone involved."

Chen looked at the folder on the table.

He looked at Justin.

He looked at Erik.

And slowly, carefully, he reached for the folder and began to read.

The information Chen provided was extraordinary.

Not just Ridgewater. A dozen other entities—shell companies, trusts, investment vehicles—all connected to the same network. Names that Justin recognized and names he didn't. A web of financial transactions that spanned continents and touched industries that ranged from real estate to pharmaceuticals to, improbably, a chain of organic grocery stores in the Pacific Northwest.

"They're everywhere," Justin said, reviewing the documents in their hotel room that night. "This isn't just money laundering. It's infrastructure. They've built a system for moving capital that touches virtually every sector of the economy."

Erik was cross-referencing the new information with data they'd obtained from Kozlov.

"The grocery stores are interesting," he said.

"How so?"

"Clean business. Legitimate customers. Steady cash flow. Perfect for—"

"Cleaning money that can't be traced."

"Exactly."

Justin stood and walked to the window. The Wilmington skyline glittered in the darkness—a small city, unremarkable by most measures, but home to some of the most sophisticated financial engineering on the planet.

"We're going to need help," he said.

"From whom?"

"Gerald Morrison. The analyst who writes the memos nobody reads."

Erik raised an eyebrow. "You want to involve oversight?"

"I want to involve someone who understands patterns. Someone who can see connections that we might miss." Justin turned from the window. "Morrison's been watching us for years. He knows more about what we do than almost anyone. And more importantly, he cares about the work—not about the bureaucracy, not about the politics, just about the work."

"Can we trust him?"

Justin considered the question.

"I think he's someone who does the right thing even when no one is watching. The kind of person who writes 2,847 memos that no one reads because he believes the record matters."

"That's either admirable or insane."

"Probably both." Justin smiled. "Sound familiar?"

Erik's expression shifted—not quite warmth, but something close.

"When do we reach out?"

"Tomorrow. Tonight, we rest. Tomorrow, we start pulling on threads."

Erik nodded and returned to his analysis.

Justin stayed by the window, watching the city, thinking about lines and money and the endless patience required to dismantle something that had taken decades to build.

It would take time.

But they had time.

And more importantly, they had purpose.

ETHICS COMMITTEE—SUPPLEMENTAL REPORT

SUBJECT: Domestic Operations—Preliminary Findings

STATUS: Concerning

The Committee has been informed of recent activities in the Delaware region involving Agents Lampert and Block. While full details remain unavailable (as usual), preliminary reports suggest:

1. Contact was made with representatives of a domestic law firm

>

2. Information was exchanged through means that may or may not have complied with applicable regulations

>

3. The phrase "the line has been crossed" was reportedly used, which we have come to recognize as an indicator of imminent complications

We note that domestic operations present unique challenges, including but not limited to:

- *Jurisdictional concerns*

>

- *Constitutional protections*

>

- *The general expectation that American citizens will not be subjected to the same treatment as foreign nationals*

The Committee recommends:

- *Enhanced oversight of all domestic activities*

>

- *Clear documentation of methods employed*

>

- *Psychological evaluation of all involved parties*

We acknowledge that these recommendations will likely be ignored.

We are placing them on record anyway.

ADDENDUM: When asked for comment, Agent Lampert reportedly responded: "Delaware isn't a real place, so technically this doesn't count as domestic."

We are choosing not to engage with this argument.

CHAPTER 7

The Rules

Every organization has rules.

The intelligence community had thousands of them—regulations governing everything from document handling to expense reports to the proper procedure for requisitioning office supplies. Most of these rules existed because someone, somewhere, had done something stupid, and the bureaucracy had responded by creating a form to prevent that stupidity from recurring.

Justin and Erik had their own rules.

Not the official ones. The real ones.

The ones that determined whether they took an operation or declined it, whether they used force or persuasion, whether they held the line or let it move.

"We should write them down," Erik said one evening.

They were in the safe house in Prague, reviewing files for an operation that was two weeks away. The target was a human trafficking network in Romania. The methods they would use were still being debated.

"Write what down?"

"The rules. Our principles. The things we won't do."

Justin looked up from his file.

"We know what we won't do."

"We know. But will the people who come after us know?"

That gave Justin pause.

They had never discussed succession before—had never acknowledged that there might be a time when they couldn't do this work anymore. But Erik's question suggested that he was thinking about it.

That he was preparing for it.

They spent the next three days writing the rules.

Not regulations—nothing as rigid as that. More like principles. Guidelines. The accumulated wisdom of decades of work, distilled into something that could be passed down.

Rule One: Never harm an innocent person.

This seemed obvious, but it wasn't. In their world, innocence was complicated. People who looked guilty were sometimes innocent. People who looked innocent were sometimes guilty. The rule required constant judgment, constant assessment, constant willingness to admit when you were wrong.

"What about collateral damage?" Erik asked. "What about the people who get hurt because they're in the wrong place at the wrong time?"

"Minimize it," Justin said. "Accept that it will sometimes happen. Take responsibility when it does."

"That's not a clear rule."

"No. But clear rules don't exist in our business."

Rule Two: Always give the target a choice.

This was Justin's rule—one he had insisted on since the beginning. Before violence, before consequences, there had to be a chance for the target to change course. To walk away. To choose a different path.

"Most of them don't take the choice," Erik observed.

"Most of them don't. But some do. And the ones who do—" Justin paused. "—they prove that people can change. That the work isn't just about punishment. It's about possibility."

Rule Three: The line is not negotiable.

This was the core of everything they did. The fundamental principle that separated them from the people they hunted.

Some things were unacceptable.

Some actions could not be excused, explained, or justified.

The line existed, and crossing it had consequences.

"But who decides where the line is?" Erik asked.

"We do. Every time. Every operation. Every choice."

"That's a lot of responsibility."

"Yes. It is."

Rule Four: Documentation matters.

This was Gerald's contribution—the principle he had been living by for decades. Every operation should be recorded. Every decision should be explained. Every action should leave a trail.

Not for legal reasons. Not for bureaucratic compliance.

Because the record mattered.

Because someday, someone would want to understand how they had made their choices. What they had considered. What they had sacrificed.

The documentation was for them.

Rule Five: The work never ends.

This was the hardest rule to accept.

There would always be more targets. More networks. More people crossing lines that shouldn't be crossed. The work wasn't a problem that could be solved—it was a condition that had to be managed.

"Doesn't that feel hopeless?" Erik asked.

"Sometimes. But think about it from the other direction. The work never ends because the need never ends. As long as people are hurting other people, there's a place for us."

"That's either comforting or depressing."

"It's both. Like everything else in this business."

They finished the document at 3 AM on the fourth night.

Five rules. Twelve pages of explanation. The accumulated wisdom of two men who had spent their lives doing the impossible.

"Is this enough?" Erik asked.

"It's a start." Justin looked at the pages they had produced. "The rest can't be written down. It has to be learned. Experienced. Earned."

"Then why bother with the document?"

"Because without something to start from, the people who come after us will have to figure everything out from scratch. They'll make mistakes we already made. They'll learn lessons we already learned."

He set down the document.

"This gives them a foundation. What they build on it is up to them."

ETHICS COMMITTEE—DOCUMENT ANALYSIS

The Committee has acquired a copy of an internal document apparently authored by Agents Lampert and Block.

The document is titled "Principles for Operations" and contains a series of guidelines that the agents appear to follow when conducting their work.

Analysis:

The document is remarkable for several reasons:

> *1. It acknowledges the existence of ethical boundaries that constrain operational activity*

>

> *2. It emphasizes the importance of documentation and accountability*

>

> *3. It recognizes the psychological toll of the work and includes provisions for self-assessment*

The Committee notes that these principles align, in many ways, with the values we have been attempting to promote through official channels.

We also note that Lampert and Block have been following these principles for decades while ignoring our formal recommendations.

Recommendation: Adopt the Lampert/Block framework as unofficial guidance for future operations.

Note: This recommendation will likely be ignored. But we are placing it on record because that is what we do. Because the record matters. Because, as the document itself states, "someday, someone will want to understand."

The document was never officially distributed.

But copies appeared in unexpected places. Training facilities. Analyst offices. The desks of young operatives who were just beginning to understand what the work required.

No one knew how the copies spread.

No one asked.

The principles became part of the culture—unwritten but understood, unofficial but influential. A foundation that shaped the thinking of everyone who encountered it.

The rules of a game that most people didn't know was being played.

Years later, Rachel Torres found a copy of the document in Gerald Morrison's personal effects.

She read it three times.

Then she started writing her own version—an update, an expansion, a continuation of the work that Justin and Erik had begun.

Not replacement. Evolution.

The line moved forward.

The rules adapted.

But the core remained the same:

Some things are unacceptable.

Consequences must exist.

The record matters.

The work never ends.

"How do you know you're doing the right thing?" a young operative asked Rachel once.

She thought about the question for a long time.

"You don't," she said finally. "Not always. Not completely. But you follow the principles. You trust the process. You accept that doubt is part of the job."

"That's not very reassuring."

"No. But it's honest." Rachel smiled. "The people who are certain they're doing the right thing—those are the ones you should worry about. The rest of us just do the best we can."

"Is that enough?"

Rachel looked out the window at a city full of people who would never know what she did.

"It has to be," she said. "Because it's all we have."

PART TWO

The Observer

"Every operation has an observer. Most of them are ours. Some of them are not."

— Internal Assessment, [REDACTED] Division

"The question isn't whether someone is watching. The question is whether they understand what they're seeing."

— Erik Block, debriefing transcript

CHAPTER 8

The Watcher

Somewhere else. Someone watching.

Dr. Alaric Voss received the report at 3:47 AM, which was when he received most things that mattered.

He didn't sleep much. Sleep was inefficient—hours of consciousness surrendered to biological necessity, time that could be spent understanding. And understanding was what Voss did. What he had always done. What he would continue doing until the patterns of human behavior surrendered their secrets to his analysis.

The report was thin. Two pages. The kind of brevity that suggested either incompetence or something genuinely unusual.

It was the latter.

Subject A and Subject B, the report began, because Voss's people didn't use names until names became necessary. *Operational pattern analysis attached. Summary: anomalous.*

Voss read the word three times.

Anomalous.

In twenty-three years of studying human behavior—of building models that predicted how people would act, what they would choose, where they would break—he had learned to distrust that word. "Anomalous" usually meant "we didn't look hard enough." It meant someone had made assumptions, cut corners, failed to account for variables that a more rigorous analysis would have captured.

But the data attached to this report was rigorous. Voss had trained these analysts himself. They didn't use words like "anomalous" unless they meant it.

He read the operational summaries.

A money laundering network in Cyprus, dismantled in eleven days. The approach had been... unusual. Direct confrontation where subtlety was expected. Psychological leverage that didn't appear in any training manual. Results that exceeded reasonable projections by a factor of three.

A trafficking operation in the Balkans, destroyed in a single night. Seventeen arrests, zero casualties among the victims, minimal collateral damage. The efficiency was striking. The precision was unnerving.

A series of smaller operations across Europe and Asia. Each one following the same pattern: identification, investigation, confrontation, resolution. Clean. Fast. Effective.

And completely outside any official structure Voss could identify.

He pulled up his models—the predictive frameworks he had spent decades refining. He fed in the data points: operational tempo, target selection, methodology, outcomes.

The models returned an error.

Not a failure to predict. An inability to categorize.

Subject A and Subject B did not fit any existing profile. They were not government operatives—their methods were too irregular. They were not mercenaries—their target selection showed moral consistency rather than financial motivation. They were not vigilantes in any conventional sense—their capabilities exceeded what individuals could develop alone.

They were something else.

Something Voss had not encountered before.

He made a phone call.

"The report on the Cyprus network," he said. "I want everything. Surveillance footage. Communication intercepts. Financial traces. Everything."

A pause on the other end. "That operation was closed. The relevant agencies—"

"I don't care about the relevant agencies. I care about understanding what I'm looking at."

Another pause. Longer this time.

"It will take resources. Attention from people who might ask questions."

"Then be careful." Voss looked out at the city below—millions of people living predictable lives, making predictable choices, following patterns he had mapped years ago. "But get me the information."

He hung up.

The models were wrong. That meant his understanding was incomplete. And incomplete understanding was unacceptable.

Voss opened a new file on his computer.

He labeled it: *PROJECT CALIBRATION.*

And he began to plan.

Six months later, he would learn their names.

Justin Lampert. Erik Block.

But by then, he would already know far more than their names.

He would know their patterns, their methods, their vulnerabilities.

He would know exactly how to test them.

And testing, Voss believed, was the first step toward understanding.

Understanding was the first step toward control.

CHAPTER 9

How Erik Sees

The hotel room in Bangkok was seventeen steps from the door to the window.

Erik knew this because he had counted them—not consciously, not deliberately, but in the automatic way his mind catalogued everything. Exits. Sight lines. The structural weakness in the ceiling that suggested water damage. The pattern of footsteps in the hallway that told him the adjacent room was occupied by a couple, probably arguing, definitely not a threat.

Justin was asleep in the other bed. Justin could sleep anywhere, in any situation, with the casual confidence of someone who trusted the world to keep turning.

Erik couldn't.

Three AM in Bangkok. The city was still loud—traffic and music and the ambient noise of twelve million people living on top of each other. But the hotel room was quiet, and in the quiet, Erik's mind did what it always did.

It replayed.

Anna's face. The last time he'd seen her—not the moment of her death, which he hadn't witnessed, but the morning before. She'd been drinking coffee and reading something on her tablet, and she'd looked up at him with that expression she had, the one that said she saw past the mask to the person underneath.

"You're thinking too loud," she'd said.

"I'm not thinking at all."

"Liar." She'd smiled. "Come here. Stop planning the next three disasters and just be here for a minute."

He'd gone. He'd sat beside her. He'd let himself be present in a way that didn't come naturally, that felt like holding his breath against the current of his own mind.

"Better," she'd said.

It had been better. For a moment.

Erik understood himself well enough to know that he was not a normal person.

Not in the ways that mattered socially. He could mimic normalcy—could smile at appropriate times, could make small talk when required, could perform the rituals of ordinary human interaction with sufficient competence that most people never noticed anything was off.

But underneath the performance, his mind was always working. Always cataloguing. Always running scenarios and calculating probabilities and preparing for threats that might never materialize.

Justin called it "being ready."

Anna had called it "being haunted."

Erik called it being Erik.

The file on the nightstand contained their next operation. A trafficking network with connections to local government, protected by corruption and violence and the particular indifference of people who had decided that some problems weren't worth solving.

Erik had read it three times. Had memorized the key details. Had already begun constructing the operational framework in his mind—entry points, extraction routes, the sequence of pressures that would collapse the network with minimum collateral damage.

Justin would read the file in the morning. Would ask questions. Would contribute ideas that Erik hadn't considered, because Justin thought differently—laterally, creatively, in ways that complemented Erik's more systematic approach.

That was why they worked.

Not because they were the same. Because they were different in ways that fit together.

Erik got up. Walked to the window. Looked out at Bangkok.

Seventeen steps.

His grandmother had taught him to play chess when he was seven. She'd been a formidable player—had competed in tournaments in her youth, before the war, before everything changed. She'd taught him that the board was a conversation, not a battle.

"The pieces don't want to win," she'd said, moving her knight. "They want to find their purpose. Your job is to help them."

He hadn't thought about her in years. Hadn't let himself. But tonight, looking out at Bangkok, he remembered the weight of the wooden pieces in his small hands. The smell of her apartment—tea and old books and something floral he'd never identified. The way she'd let him win sometimes, and the way she'd crushed him other times, because she believed children should learn that losing was survivable.

He still played, occasionally. Online, against strangers, under a name that wasn't his. Not to win. Just to feel the conversation again. To remember that some patterns were beautiful instead of dangerous.

Somewhere in this city, people were being bought and sold. Children were being taken from families. Lives were being destroyed for profit by men who had calculated that human suffering was an acceptable cost of doing business.

Tomorrow, he and Justin would begin the process of imposing consequences.

Not justice—Erik had stopped believing in justice years ago. Justice implied a system, a framework, a structure that weighed outcomes and determined appropriate responses.

What they did wasn't justice. It was simpler than that.

It was the line.

Anna had understood. That was the thing about her that Erik had loved most—not her beauty, not her intelligence, not even her kindness, though she had all of those. It was her understanding.

"You don't do this because you enjoy it," she'd said once. "You do it because you can't not do it. Because once you've seen certain things, you can't pretend you haven't seen them."

"That makes me sound obsessive."

"It makes you sound human." She'd touched his face. "The best kind of human. The kind that feels responsible even when no one asked them to be."

"Is that a compliment?"

"It's an observation." She'd smiled. "I love you, Erik. All of you. Even the parts that don't sleep and can't stop planning and see threats in every shadow."

"There are threats in every shadow."

"I know. That's why I'm glad you're the one looking for them."

She was gone now.

Gone because he hadn't been there. Gone because the one night he'd let himself relax, let himself believe that the world could wait, the world hadn't waited.

Erik didn't blame himself for her death. Not anymore. He'd worked through that particular darkness in the months after, had come to understand that guilt was just another form of arrogance—the belief that he could have controlled outcomes that were never in his control.

But he remembered.

And remembering meant that every operation, every target, every moment when he chose to act instead of wait, was touched by her absence.

Not revenge. Erik had given up revenge when the last of the people directly responsible for her death had been dealt with.

This was something else.

This was becoming the person she had believed he could be.

Justin stirred in the other bed.

"You're awake," he said. Not a question.

"Yes."

"You've been staring out that window for—" Justin checked his phone. "—forty-seven minutes."

"I was thinking."

"About?"

Erik didn't answer immediately. The question deserved consideration.

"About why we do this," he said finally. "About what it costs. About whether the cost is worth it."

Justin sat up. His face was serious in the dim light.

"Is it?"

"I don't know." Erik turned from the window. "But I know that not doing it costs more. I know that the alternative—watching, knowing, doing nothing—that's a kind of death too. Slower. Quieter. But death all the same."

"That's very philosophical for four AM."

"I'm a philosophical person."

"You're a person who pretends to be simple so that other people underestimate you."

Erik almost smiled.

"Is it working?"

"On most people." Justin lay back down. "Not on me. Never on me."

"I know."

"Good." Justin closed his eyes. "Now stop thinking so loud and let me sleep. We have a network to dismantle tomorrow."

Erik looked back out the window.

Seventeen steps from the door.

Tomorrow, they would begin.

Tonight, he would watch the city and let his mind do what it always did—plan, prepare, protect.

It was who he was.

It was who he chose to be.

And somewhere out there, the people who thought they were untouchable had no idea what was coming for them.

Anna had been right about one thing.

The best humans were the ones who felt responsible even when no one asked them to be.

Erik felt responsible.

That was going to be a problem for a lot of people.

CHAPTER 10

The Vegas Incident

Las Vegas was a city built on lies.

Not the usual lies—not the small deceptions people told themselves to get through the day. Vegas dealt in bigger lies. The lie that luck was real. The lie that the next hand would be different. The lie that a city in the desert could sustain forty million visitors a year without eventually running out of water.

Justin Lampert loved Las Vegas.

Erik Block hated it.

But they were in Las Vegas because that's where the target was. And the target was a problem.

His name was Victor Castellan, and he ran a money-laundering operation that spanned three continents. He was also in Vegas for his daughter's wedding.

"We can't do anything during the wedding," Justin said, studying the floor plans. "Too many civilians."

"The bachelor party," Erik said. "It's the only time he'll be separated from family."

Justin raised an eyebrow. "You want to crash a mobster's bachelor party?"

"I can blend in."

Justin laughed so hard he nearly fell out of his chair.

"Erik, you don't blend in. You've never blended in. You could walk into a room full of identical twins and you'd still be the one everyone noticed."

Erik looked down at his clothes. Black shirt. Black pants. Black jacket.

"I'll buy something."

Justin grinned. "This I have to see."

The club was called Apex. Thirty-seventh floor. Chandeliers worth more than most houses.

Erik walked in wearing a Hawaiian shirt.

It was bright blue with orange parrots on it. Justin had picked it out. Erik looked like he was being slowly murdered by the fabric.

"Stop touching it," Justin muttered.

"It's loud."

"That's the point."

"I can hear it judging me."

Justin had to look away to keep from laughing.

They made it past security. Castellan's party had commandeered the VIP section—leather couches, beautiful people, men with obvious bulges under their jackets.

Justin counted the security. "Eight."

"Nine," Erik corrected. "The bartender. He's watching hands, not bottles."

Justin made a mental note. Then he smiled and started walking toward the VIP section.

The approach worked. The name-drop worked. The threat about the Moldova server farm worked.

Castellan agreed to a private conversation in the back room.

They were four minutes into the meeting when Erik's phone buzzed.

He glanced at the screen. His face didn't change, but something shifted behind his eyes.

"Excuse me," he said, and stepped outside.

Justin kept talking—kept Castellan focused on the negotiation, on the threat, on the deal. But part of his mind was tracking the seconds. Thirty. Sixty. Ninety.

Erik didn't come back.

The bathroom was at the end of the hall.

Erik found the man waiting for him there—young, nervous, holding a phone with shaking hands.

"My name is Danny Reeves," the man said. "I work for Castellan. I've been working for Castellan for three years. And I need to get out."

Erik assessed him in two seconds. Early twenties. Accountant's hands. Eyes that hadn't slept in days.

"Why are you telling me this?"

"Because I saw you come in. I recognized you." Danny's voice cracked. "You're the ones who took down the Marchetti network. The Kovacs operation. You're—you're the people who do things."

"I don't know what you're talking about."

"Please." Danny grabbed his arm. "I have a daughter. She's six years old. Her name is Maria. Castellan found out I've been skimming—not much, just enough to try to get us out—and he's going to kill me. Tonight. After the party."

Erik looked at the hand on his arm.

"Let go."

Danny let go.

"I have evidence," Danny said quickly. "Everything. The full network. The connections you don't even know about. I'll give it all to you. I just need to disappear. Me and Maria."

"Where's your daughter now?"

"My mother's house. In Henderson. Twenty minutes from here."

Erik calculated. The operation was simple: extract information from Castellan, expose the network, leave. Adding a family extraction turned simple into complicated.

Complicated got people killed.

"Please," Danny whispered. "I know I'm a criminal. I know I don't deserve help. But Maria didn't do anything. She's six. She likes dinosaurs and strawberry ice cream and she doesn't know her father is a monster."

Erik thought about another child. Fourteen years old. Ukrainian. A warehouse in Gda■sk.

Some lessons cost everything to learn.

"Stay here," Erik said. "Don't move. Don't talk to anyone. When I come back, you do exactly what I say."

"You'll help us?"

Erik didn't answer. He was already walking back to the private room.

"We have a complication," Erik said, stepping back inside.

Castellan looked up sharply. Justin's eyes asked a question.

"The accountant. Danny Reeves. Castellan knows he's been skimming."

Castellan's face went cold. "That's none of your concern."

"It is now." Erik's voice was flat. "He's coming with us."

"The hell he is."

"He has a daughter. Six years old. You were going to kill him tonight and leave her an orphan."

Castellan stood. The guards at the door reached for their weapons.

"You think you can walk into my city, threaten me, and then tell me what I can and can't do with my own people?"

Justin stepped between them. "Victor. Let's think about this."

"There's nothing to think about. Reeves stole from me. There are consequences for—"

"Consequences," Erik said quietly. "Yes. There are."

He moved.

The first guard was unconscious before he understood what was happening. The second got his gun halfway out of the holster—Erik broke his wrist and used the momentum to throw him into the third. The fourth fired—the shot went wide, into the ceiling—and then Erik was there, inside his guard, and the fight was over.

Four seconds. Four guards. Zero fatalities.

Castellan hadn't moved.

"Here's what's going to happen," Erik said, straightening the ridiculous Hawaiian shirt. "You're going to let Danny Reeves walk out of here. You're going to forget he exists. And in exchange, we'll forget that you just tried to have us killed."

"You came into my house—"

"We came to offer you a deal. A good deal. Networks exposed, but you walk free. Your daughter gets married without her father in federal custody." Erik stepped closer. "That deal is still on the table. But Danny Reeves is no longer negotiable."

Castellan looked at the four unconscious guards. Looked at Justin, who hadn't moved but whose hand was now inside his jacket. Looked at Erik, standing perfectly still in a Hawaiian shirt with orange parrots, having just dismantled his security team in four seconds.

"Fine," he said. "Take the accountant. Take his family. But after tonight, I never see any of you again."

"Agreed."

They extracted Danny and Maria from Henderson at 2 AM.

The girl was still half-asleep, clutching a stuffed triceratops. She looked up at Erik with drowsy eyes.

"Are you a superhero?" she asked.

Erik glanced at his shirt. The parrots seemed to be mocking him.

"No."

"You look like a superhero. Superheroes wear bright colors."

Justin, behind him, made a sound that might have been a cough.

"Go back to sleep," Erik said.

Maria clutched her dinosaur tighter. "My daddy says we're going on an adventure."

"That's right."

"Will there be ice cream?"

Erik looked at Danny, who was pale and shaking and trying very hard not to cry.

"Yes," Erik said. "There will be ice cream."

The next morning, the FBI received an anonymous tip that led to the largest money-laundering investigation in Nevada history. Danny Reeves testified via secure video link from a location that didn't exist. His evidence brought down fifty-three members of Castellan's organization.

Castellan himself was not among those arrested.

But he never operated in Las Vegas again.

And his daughter's wedding went beautifully.

"You kept the shirt," Justin said later, on the flight to nowhere.

Erik looked at the Hawaiian monstrosity folded in his bag. The parrots stared back at him, aggressively orange.

"Maria liked it."

"Maria is six."

"She has good taste."

Justin laughed.

"You know," he said, "most operatives would have left Danny to die. Simpler. Cleaner. No complications."

"Most operatives wouldn't have to explain to a six-year-old why her father wasn't coming home."

"Is that why you did it?"

Erik was quiet for a long moment.

"I did it because some lines aren't about strategy. They're about who you want to be when you look in the mirror." He glanced at the shirt again. "Even if the mirror is full of parrots."

Justin smiled.

"That's the most words you've said in three months."

"Don't get used to it."

But Justin caught the ghost of something—almost a smile—on Erik's face.

The parrots had won.

CHAPTER 11

What Erik Couldn't Stop

Erik Block arrived seventeen minutes too late.

He knew it the moment he entered the warehouse—the particular stillness that came after violence, the copper smell that meant blood, the silence where there should have been breathing.

Justin was in Berlin, running down a financial lead. Gerald was analyzing patterns in Washington. Rachel was still three months from joining them.

This one had been Erik's.

His operation. His intelligence. His decision to move tonight instead of waiting for backup.

His failure.

The girl's name was Katya. Fourteen years old. Ukrainian. She had been taken from a bus station in Kyiv three weeks ago, moved through a pipeline that Erik had been tracking for two months.

He had the network mapped. He had the locations. He had everything except time.

"Move tomorrow," Justin had said on the phone six hours ago. "We can be there in eighteen hours. Do it together."

"Tomorrow might be too late. They're rotating the holding sites. If we lose track of her—"

"Then we find her again. Erik, this isn't a solo operation. The security profile—"

"I can handle the security."

A pause. Justin's voice careful.

"I know you can. That's not what worries me."

"What worries you?"

"That you want to handle it alone."

Erik had gone anyway.

Not because he thought Justin was wrong. Because he couldn't accept the alternative—couldn't accept waiting eighteen hours while a fourteen-year-old girl moved further into a system designed to destroy her.

The facility was a converted factory on the outskirts of Gda■sk. Four guards. Standard rotation. Security that looked professional but had gaps if you knew where to look.

Erik knew where to look.

He was inside in nine minutes. Past the guards in another four. Moving through corridors that smelled like concrete and fear, checking rooms that were empty or contained people he couldn't save—not tonight, not alone, but people whose faces he memorized for later.

The holding room was on the third floor. Door reinforced. Lock sophisticated.

Forty-seven seconds to bypass.

He opened the door and found her.

Katya had been dead for approximately two hours.

The medical details didn't matter. What mattered was this: she had been alive when Erik started his approach. Alive when he was bypassing the perimeter security. Alive when he was moving through the corridors.

She had died while he was fifty meters away.

Erik stood in the doorway and understood something about himself that he had been avoiding for years.

He was very good at what he did. Good enough to infiltrate facilities alone, to neutralize threats without backup, to do things that should have been impossible.

But being good wasn't the same as being fast enough.

Being capable wasn't the same as being there in time.

He called Justin from the roof.

"It's done."

"The girl?"

Erik didn't answer immediately. He was looking out at Gda■sk—the lights of a city where people were sleeping, eating dinner, living lives that didn't include rooms where fourteen-year-olds died alone.

"Erik."

"She was dead when I got there. Two hours. Maybe less."

Silence on the line.

"I was fifty meters away," Erik continued. "Fifty meters and two hours. If I'd been faster—"

"You couldn't have known."

"I should have been faster."

"Erik—"

"I need to finish here. The guards saw me. They'll move the others. I need to—"

"Leave. Now. Come to Berlin."

"I can still—"

"You can still get yourself killed trying to make up for something that isn't your fault." Justin's voice was sharp. Then softer: "Come to Berlin. We'll go back together. We'll shut the whole network down. But not tonight. Not alone."

Erik looked at the city.

"Okay," he said.

He didn't mean it. But he said it anyway.

He stayed.

Not because he had a plan. Because leaving felt like abandonment. Because somewhere in this city, the people who had killed Katya were still breathing, and Erik wasn't ready to let them keep breathing.

He found three of them that night.

The things he did to them were not in any training manual. Were not sanctioned by any authority. Were not, by any reasonable measure, proportionate.

They were precise.

They were thorough.

They were the only language Erik knew how to speak when the words ran out.

Justin found him the next morning, sitting in a café near the train station, drinking coffee he didn't taste.

"The network?" Justin asked, sitting down across from him.

"Disrupted. Temporarily. They'll rebuild in a few months."

"The men?"

"Alive." Erik looked at his hands. "Damaged. But alive."

"I told you to come to Berlin."

"I know."

"I told you not to do this alone."

"I know."

Justin didn't say anything else for a long moment. The café was busy—morning commuters, tourists, people who lived in a world where girls didn't die in warehouses.

"Katya's family," Erik said finally. "I found them. Her mother works in a hospital in Kyiv. Her father is dead—accident, three years ago. She has a younger brother."

"Erik—"

"I need to tell them something. I don't know what. But I need to tell them something."

Justin studied his partner. The flatness in his voice. The stillness that wasn't calm but something else—something colder.

"We'll tell them together," Justin said. "We'll tell them we found the people responsible. We'll tell them there were consequences."

"Is that enough?"

"No." Justin signaled for coffee. "But it's what we have."

They went to Kyiv three days later.

Erik sat in a small apartment and told a mother that her daughter was dead. That the people who took her had been found. That they would never take anyone else's daughter.

The mother didn't cry. She sat very still, the way people do when the grief is too big to express, and asked only one question.

"Did she suffer?"

Erik lied.

"No," he said. "It was quick. She didn't suffer."

It was the kindest thing he knew how to do.

Justin waited outside.

When Erik emerged, his face was the same as always—controlled, still, unreadable. But something had shifted behind his eyes. Something that would take years to fully understand.

"I'm not going to do that again," Erik said.

"Do what?"

95

"Go alone. Decide alone. Fail alone." He looked at Justin. "Anna used to say that the only way to survive the work was to not do it alone. I thought I understood what she meant. I didn't."

"And now?"

Erik didn't answer immediately.

"Now I know what it costs," he said. "Not the work itself. The arrogance of thinking I could carry it without help."

They walked in silence for a while.

"The network," Justin said eventually. "The one that took Katya. Gerald found more connections. It's bigger than we thought."

"How much bigger?"

"International. Sophisticated. Someone's running it who knows how to avoid attention."

Erik nodded.

"Then we take it apart. Together."

"Together," Justin agreed.

It was the beginning of the thread that would eventually lead them to Alaric Voss.

Neither of them knew that yet.

But they knew one thing: the work was too big for one person. The line was too long to hold alone.

Some lessons cost everything to learn.

Katya had paid the price for this one.

Erik would spend the rest of his life trying to make that payment mean something.

CHAPTER 12

Gerald's Decision

[To be inserted after the Hong Kong operation]

Gerald Morrison did something he had never done in twenty-three years of government service.

He deleted a report.

Not his own report—that would have been detectable, auditable, the kind of thing that ended careers. No, he deleted someone else's report. An analyst in a sister agency who had gotten too close to the truth about what Justin Lampert and Erik Block actually did.

The analyst had written a memo suggesting "enhanced surveillance" and "potential intervention." The analyst had recommended that "assets be deployed to assess the threat level posed by these rogue operators."

Gerald deleted the memo.

Then he deleted the backup.

Then he called in a favor from a friend in IT security and made sure the deletion couldn't be traced.

He sat in his office for a long time after, Theodore purring on the desk beside him, wondering what he had just become.

For twenty-three years, he had been the reader. The watcher. The man who saw everything and did nothing except file reports that nobody read. He had told himself that was enough. That documentation mattered. That someday, someone would look at his records and understand what had really happened.

But documentation didn't save anyone.

Documentation didn't stop the networks or rescue the children or impose consequences on people who thought they were untouchable.

Justin and Erik did that.

And Gerald had just made a choice to protect them.

"I'm not sure when it happened," he muttered. "The moment I stopped being an observer and started being… something else."

"They're doing good work. Real work. The kind of work I've been writing reports about for two decades without ever actually helping."

He scratched behind the cat's ears.

"Maybe that's enough justification. Maybe it isn't. But I made the choice, and now I have to live with it."

He looked at the screen where the deleted memo had been.

"I think I'm going to make more choices like this," he said quietly. "I think I'm going to help them. Really help them. Not just watch and document—actually do something."

Theodore yawned.

"You're right," Gerald said. "It's terrifying. But it's also the first time in twenty-three years that I've felt like my work actually mattered."

He turned back to his screens.

Somewhere out there, Justin and Erik were doing impossible things. And Gerald Morrison—career bureaucrat, professional observer, the man who read the reports—was going to help them do it.

He started building the network that would, eighteen months later, bring down Alaric Voss.

He didn't know that yet.

CHAPTER 13

The Ones They Didn't Save

The Weight

David Chen was an accountant.

That's what people said when they talked about him, which wasn't often. He worked at a mid-size firm in Cleveland. He had a wife named Linda, two kids—Marcus, twelve, and Sarah, nine—and a house in a neighborhood that was nice enough to feel safe but not nice enough to feel guilty about.

He drove a Honda Civic. He coached his son's baseball team on weekends. He did his neighbors' taxes for free because it was easier than explaining why he couldn't.

He was, by every measurable standard, ordinary.

The kind of person who disappeared into the statistics of a city. The kind of person that systems were designed to process without noticing.

And that's why no one expected him to notice.

The discrepancy was small.

A rounding error in a quarterly report. The kind of thing that most people would attribute to human error, software glitches, or the general entropy of numbers moving through systems designed by committees.

David Chen didn't attribute it to any of those things.

He attributed it to theft.

Not the dramatic kind—no one was walking out with bags of money. This was the quiet kind. The systematic kind. Small amounts skimmed from hundreds of transactions, routed through accounts that existed only on paper, accumulating into something substantial without ever becoming obvious.

David had a gift for noticing patterns. Had since he was a child, solving puzzles that his teachers thought were too advanced, finding shortcuts through problems that other people brute-forced.

The pattern he found in the quarterly report was subtle. Elegant, almost. Someone had designed it carefully—someone who understood how accounting systems worked, who knew which checks were performed and which were skipped, who had mapped the terrain of corporate oversight and found every gap.

But they hadn't accounted for David Chen.

They hadn't accounted for the accountant who actually paid attention.

David spent three weeks documenting it.

Three weeks of late nights and locked doors and the growing certainty that he was looking at something he wasn't supposed to see. He told Linda he was working on a project. He told the kids he'd make it up to them. He told himself that this was the right thing to do.

The file grew.

Page after page of evidence. Transaction records. Bank statements. Shell company registrations. A web of connections that led from his firm to three other firms, two banks, and a pension fund that managed retirement savings for 40,000 people.

Forty thousand people whose money was being stolen, slowly, systematically, by people who thought they were too clever to get caught.

When the file was complete—sixty-seven pages, meticulously organized, backed up in three different locations—David Chen had a choice.

He could delete everything. Pretend he'd never seen it. Continue his small but solid life.

Or he could do something.

He thought about Marcus and Sarah. About the kind of world he wanted them to grow up in. About what it meant to be a person who saw something wrong and did nothing.

He made copies.

He contacted the authorities.

He became a witness.

The meeting with the FBI was scheduled for Tuesday.

David Chen never made it.

Justin and Erik learned about David Chen the way they learned about most things: too late.

The file arrived in their inbox on a Wednesday morning—passed through channels that didn't officially exist, flagged by an algorithm that looked for patterns suggesting someone had tried to do the right thing and had been punished for it.

David Chen, accountant. Cleveland, Ohio. Three days missing. No body recovered. Family relocated under protective custody.

Justin read the file twice.

"We missed it," he said.

The words hung in the air. Heavy. Accusatory. The kind of words that couldn't be taken back or excused away.

Erik was already pulling up secondary documentation—phone records, financial transfers, the digital footprint of a man who had tried to expose corruption and had been erased for it.

"The timeline was impossible," Erik said. "He filed his report on Friday. By Monday, they knew. By Tuesday—"

"By Tuesday, they moved." Justin's voice was flat. "Professional job. No traces. Clean extraction."

"Too clean."

Justin nodded. "They had help. Someone inside."

He pulled up a name—a name that had appeared in three other files over the past year, always at the edges, never in the center.

"Voss," he said.

Erik looked at the screen.

"He's an advisor. A consultant. He doesn't get his hands dirty."

"He doesn't have to." Justin stood, pacing the small room they were using as a temporary base. "He designs the systems. Sets up the protocols. Makes sure that when someone like David Chen finds something they shouldn't, there's already a plan in place."

"A plan we couldn't see."

"A plan we didn't look for." Justin's hands clenched. "Because we were in Madrid, dealing with the Cortez situation, while a man in Cleveland was dying for doing his job."

Erik was quiet.

There was nothing to say. Nothing that would make it better.

David Chen was dead because they hadn't been paying attention. Because the world was too big and their reach was too small and sometimes—sometimes—the bad guys won.

"The family," Erik said finally. "Linda. The kids."

"Protected. FBI has them in a safe house."

"For now."

Justin nodded. "For now."

They both knew what that meant. Safe houses weren't permanent. Protection faded. Memories shortened. And the people who had killed David Chen would remember that there were witnesses. Would remember that Linda Chen knew things, had seen things, could potentially identify things.

The danger wasn't over.

It had just gone quiet.

The funeral was held on a Saturday.

There was no body to bury—the FBI hadn't found one, and probably never would—but Linda Chen had insisted on a service anyway. A chance to say goodbye. A chance to tell her children that their father had been a hero, even if the world would never know.

The church was small. Catholic. The kind of place that smelled like old wood and older faith.

Justin attended.

He stood in the back, wearing a suit he didn't like and an expression that revealed nothing. He watched Linda Chen hold her children's hands. Watched Marcus, twelve years old, try to be strong. Watched Sarah, nine, cry in the way children cry when they don't understand why something terrible has happened.

The priest spoke about courage. About doing the right thing. About the rewards that awaited in the next life for those who suffered in this one.

Justin listened and said nothing.

He didn't believe in the next life.

He barely believed in this one.

After the service, he approached Linda.

"Mrs. Chen."

She looked at him with eyes that had cried themselves empty. She was a small woman, tired, wearing black that didn't fit quite right because she had bought it the day before and hadn't had time to alter it.

"I don't know you."

"No," Justin agreed. "You don't. But I knew about your husband. What he did. Why he did it."

Linda's face hardened.

"Everyone knows what he did. It's been on the news. 'Accountant Disappears After Reporting Fraud.' They made him sound naive. Like he didn't know what he was getting into."

"He knew," Justin said quietly. "He filed that report anyway. That's not naive. That's brave."

Linda's eyes filled with tears.

"Brave got him killed."

"Yes. It did. And I'm sorry. I'm sorry we didn't see it coming. I'm sorry we weren't there."

Linda stared at him.

"Who are you?"

"Someone who should have been paying attention." Justin reached into his pocket and pulled out a card. Blank. No name. Just a phone number. "If you ever need anything—if you ever feel unsafe, if anyone contacts you, if something seems wrong—call this number. Day or night."

Linda took the card. Looked at it. Looked at him.

"What happens when I call?"

Justin managed a tired smile.

"Help arrives."

He walked away before she could ask more questions.

He had nothing else to offer her. No explanations that would make sense. No comfort that would ease the grief.

Just a promise.

And promises, in his experience, were the only currency that mattered.

Erik found the connection in Rotterdam.

The shipping company was a front—one of dozens that Voss had established over the years, each one designed to move money, information, and occasionally people in ways that couldn't be traced.

He tracked the connection to a warehouse. To a server. To a name that had been mentioned in passing in the Chen file but had seemed too peripheral to matter.

It wasn't peripheral.

It was central.

And when Erik pulled the thread, the entire tapestry began to unravel.

The men who had killed David Chen were professionals.

They had training. Resources. Protection.

They had been doing this for years—cleaning up problems, eliminating witnesses, ensuring that people like David Chen never got the chance to cause trouble.

They had everything except the one thing that might have saved them:

An understanding of what happens when Erik Block decides to make something his problem.

Justin got the call at 3 AM.

"It's done," Erik said.

"All of them?"

"All of them."

Justin didn't respond immediately. Outside his window, the city slept. Or pretended to. Cities never really slept—they just got quieter.

"Did they talk?"

"One of them. Before the end."

"And?"

"Voss gave the order. But he didn't design the operation. Someone else did. Someone higher."

Justin closed his eyes.

"Do we have a name?"

"Not yet. But we have a trail."

"Then we follow it."

"Yes."

The line went dead.

Justin sat in the dark for a long time, thinking about David Chen. About the file that had started everything. About the sixty-seven pages of evidence that had cost a man his life.

David Chen had been an accountant. Ordinary. Unremarkable. The kind of person that systems were designed to ignore.

But he had seen something wrong, and he had tried to fix it.

And even though he had failed—even though he had died—his work hadn't been for nothing.

The file survived.

The evidence remained.

The network he'd exposed was collapsing, piece by piece, as Justin and Erik followed the trails he had uncovered.

It wasn't justice.

Justice would be David Chen alive, playing baseball with his son, doing his neighbors' taxes, living the ordinary life he had earned.

This wasn't justice.

But it was something.

Three days later, Justin Lampert set up a trust fund.

Anonymous. Untraceable. Enough to put Marcus and Sarah Chen through college, medical school, whatever they wanted.

It wasn't justice.

It wasn't redemption.

It was the only thing he could do.

Erik found out about it a week later. Didn't say anything. Just nodded once, in that way that meant he understood.

They never talked about it again.

But sometimes, late at night, Justin would check on the fund. Would see the balance grow. Would imagine Marcus Chen graduating from somewhere prestigious, becoming someone important, doing something that mattered.

It didn't make it better.

Nothing made it better.

But it was something.

And sometimes, something was all you had.

INCIDENT REPORT—OPERATION CHEN

Classification: UNSANCTIONED

Status: RESOLVED

Following the death of civilian whistleblower David Chen, Agents Lampert and Block conducted an independent investigation into the parties responsible.

Findings:

  • *Six individuals directly involved in Chen's disappearance:*
DECEASED

>

  • *Financial network supporting operation: DISMANTLED*

>

    • *Connected parties in three countries: EXPOSED*

>

      • *Total assets seized: $47 million*

>

    • *Total arrests resulting from evidence disclosure: 23*

The Committee notes that Agents Lampert and Block did not request authorization for this operation. When asked why, Agent Lampert responded: "Because David Chen didn't get to ask permission before they killed him."

This response has been noted in his file.

ADDENDUM: The Committee has received a letter from Linda Chen thanking "whoever was responsible for making sure David's death meant something." We have filed this letter under "Things We Cannot Officially Acknowledge."

Justin visited the grave six months later.

There was still no body beneath the stone, but Linda had put up a marker anyway. Something for the children to visit. Something to make the loss feel real.

The inscription read:

DAVID CHEN

>

1978—2024

>

He saw something wrong and tried to make it right.

Justin stood there for a long time.

He didn't pray. Didn't believe in it. But he made a promise—the same promise he made every time they lost someone who had tried to do the right thing.

We remember.

We don't forget.

And we don't stop.

The wind picked up, scattering leaves across the cemetery.

Justin turned and walked away.

There was more work to do. There was always more work to do.

And somewhere, in the spaces between the systems that protected the powerful, another David Chen was about to find something he shouldn't see.

Justin hoped they'd be faster this time.

He hoped they'd be there.

But hope, in his experience, was a poor substitute for vigilance.

So he kept watching.

And waiting.

And remembering the ones they didn't save.

CHAPTER 14

The Analyst Who Asked Questions

Rachel Torres had been fired three times.

The first time was from the FBI, for writing a report that contradicted her supervisor's conclusions. The report was accurate. The conclusions were politically convenient. Rachel learned that accuracy and convenience rarely coexisted.

The second time was from a private intelligence firm, for refusing to bury evidence of client misconduct. The client was a defense contractor. The misconduct involved children in a supply chain overseas. Rachel learned that money could make almost anything invisible.

The third time was from the NSA, for asking why certain patterns in financial data were being ignored. The patterns suggested systematic corruption at levels that made her supervisors uncomfortable. Rachel learned that some questions were more dangerous than any answer.

Now she was thirty-four years old, unemployable in any official capacity, and sitting in a diner in Baltimore watching two men who didn't know she existed.

She had been watching them for six weeks.

Justin Lampert entered first, scanning the room with the practiced casualness of someone who had learned to assess threats without appearing to. He was tall, well-dressed, radiating a confidence that could read as arrogance if you didn't look closely.

Rachel looked closely. She saw the micro-expressions—the slight tension around the eyes, the way his hands stayed visible but ready. This was a man who expected violence and had made peace with it.

Erik Block entered thirty seconds later, through a different door. Of course. They never used the same entrance. Rachel had noted this pattern across fourteen separate observations.

Block was harder to read. Quieter. More contained. Where Lampert filled space with presence and charm, Block seemed to absorb it—drawing attention inward, becoming less visible through sheer stillness.

They sat in a booth near the back. Good sight lines to both exits. Predictable.

Rachel waited until they had ordered coffee before approaching. "Mind if I sit?"

Lampert looked up. His expression didn't change, but something shifted behind his eyes—a calculation happening faster than conscious thought.

"The diner's mostly empty," he said. "Plenty of other seats."

"But none of them are next to you."

She sat down without waiting for permission. Block's hand moved slightly under the table. Rachel noted it, filed it away, didn't react.

"I know who you are," she said. "I know what you do. And before you decide whether to kill me, you should know that I've arranged for a detailed file to be released to seventeen news organizations if I don't check in within the next four hours."

Lampert smiled. It was not a reassuring smile.

"That's a very specific threat from someone we've never met."

"It's not a threat. It's context." Rachel pulled a folder from her bag and set it on the table. "I'm not here to expose you. I'm here to help you."

"We don't need help."

"The Cyprus operation. The network you dismantled." Rachel opened the folder, revealing a stack of documents. "You missed something."

Block spoke for the first time. "We didn't miss anything."

"You missed the backup server in Delaware. You missed the secondary financial architecture that was designed to survive exactly the kind of takedown you executed." Rachel met his eyes without flinching. "The network is rebuilding. Different names, same structure. You cut off the head, but the body is still moving."

Silence.

Lampert picked up one of the documents. Read it. His expression didn't change, but Rachel saw his jaw tighten.

"Where did you get this?"

"I'm an analyst. I analyze things." She leaned back. "I was good at my job. Too good, apparently. The kind of good that makes people nervous."

"So you got fired."

"Three times. For asking questions that had answers people didn't want to hear."

"And now you're here. Asking us questions."

"No." Rachel shook her head. "Now I'm here offering answers. And asking for something in return."

Lampert exchanged a glance with Block. The silent communication of people who had worked together long enough to develop their own language.

"What do you want?" Lampert asked.

"I want in."

"In what?"

"Whatever this is. Whatever you're doing." Rachel gestured at the folder. "I've spent fifteen years inside systems that are designed to fail. Oversight committees that don't oversee. Intelligence agencies that ignore intelligence. Ethics reviews that review everything except ethics."

She leaned forward.

"You're doing something different. You're actually holding people accountable. I want to be part of that."

"You don't know what you're asking for," Block said quietly.

"I know exactly what I'm asking for. I've read your operational files—the ones that exist, anyway. I know about Kozlov. About the networks you've dismantled. About the methods you use."

"And that doesn't bother you?"

Rachel considered the question seriously. It deserved a serious answer.

"I've seen what happens when no one is willing to do difficult things," she said. "Children in supply chains. Pension funds stolen. People trafficked across borders while agencies file reports that no one reads. I've written those reports. I've watched them disappear into filing cabinets."

She met Block's eyes.

"What you do bothers me less than what happens when no one does anything."

The silence stretched.

Lampert finished reading the documents. Set them down carefully.

"The Delaware connection," he said. "You're right. We missed it."

"I know."

"That's a significant intelligence failure on our part."

"I know that too."

"And you found it in—what? Six weeks of independent analysis?"

"Four. The other two weeks were spent finding you."

Another glance between Lampert and Block. Another silent conversation.

"You understand," Lampert said slowly, "that if you're lying to us—if this is some kind of approach, some kind of trap—"

"You'll kill me. Yes. I understood that when I sat down." Rachel didn't blink. "I also understand that you won't do it casually. You have rules. Lines. That's why I'm here instead of talking to someone else."

"There is no one else."

"I know." Rachel smiled. It was the first genuine expression she'd allowed herself. "That's the other reason I'm here. There should be someone else. There should be more people doing what you do. And maybe—if I can prove myself—I can be one of them."

Block was very still.

"What do you think?" Lampert asked him.

Block studied Rachel for a long moment. Reading her the way he read rooms, the way he read situations, the way he read everything.

"She's telling the truth," he said finally.

"How do you know?"

"Because she's terrified." Block's voice was soft. "And she sat down anyway."

Rachel hadn't realized she was trembling until Block named it. The fear had been there all along—coiled beneath the bravado, beneath the careful preparation, beneath the calculated risk of approaching two of the most dangerous people she had ever identified.

But she had sat down anyway.

Because some things mattered more than fear.

"The Delaware server," Lampert said. "Show us everything you have."

Rachel opened the folder wider.

And began to prove herself.

CHAPTER 15

The Ones They Did

A Counterweight

Sarah Okonkwo had never planned to be brave.

She had planned to be comfortable. A mid-level position at a respectable firm. A house in a decent neighborhood. A daughter she could send to good schools. A life that was small but solid, built on small but solid choices.

She had grown up in Lagos, moved to London for university, and somehow ended up in a cubicle in Chicago, processing financial reports for a company that made components for medical devices. It wasn't glamorous. It wasn't exciting. But it was stable, and stability was something Sarah had learned to value.

Then she had seen the file.

It was an accident.

A misfiled document that ended up on her desk instead of someone else's. She should have sent it back immediately. She should have pretended she hadn't seen it.

Instead, she read it.

And what she read changed everything.

The file contained evidence of systematic fraud. Not the small, deniable kind—the kind you could attribute to mistakes or misunderstandings. This was deliberate. This was organized. This was a machine designed to steal money from people who couldn't afford to lose it.

Pension funds. Retirement accounts. The life savings of people who had worked for decades, trusting that the system would protect them.

All of it being siphoned away, slowly, systematically, by people who thought they were too clever to get caught.

Sarah had a choice.

She could send the file back, pretend she'd never seen it, and continue her small but solid life.

Or she could do something.

She thought about Maya. Eight years old. Too young to understand corruption, too old to be protected from its consequences. She thought about the kind of world she wanted her daughter to grow up in. About what it meant to be a person who saw something wrong and did nothing.

She made copies.

She contacted the authorities.

She became a witness.

The safe house was a three-bedroom apartment in a building that looked like every other building on the street.

Bland walls. Functional furniture. The kind of place that was designed to be forgotten.

Sarah sat in the living room and watched her daughter play with blocks. They had brought Maya's blocks from home—one of the few things they'd been allowed to take. Everything else had been left behind in the rush of the move, the urgency of getting somewhere safe.

Maya was building a castle. She was very serious about it.

"Mommy?" Maya asked, not looking up from her construction. "When are we going home?"

Sarah smiled. It was a tired smile. A scared smile. But she made sure Maya couldn't see the scared part.

"Soon, baby. Soon."

"How soon?"

"Soon enough."

Maya accepted this, the way children accept things they don't understand. She went back to her blocks.

Sarah watched her and tried not to cry.

The handlers came twice a day.

Different faces, but always the same careful professionalism. They brought food. They brought updates. They brought reassurances that felt less reassuring each time.

"You're doing the right thing," one of them told her. Agent Morrison, his name was. He had kind eyes and a nervous habit of checking his phone. "The information you've provided—it's going to make a difference."

"I know," Sarah said.

"A real difference. People are going to be held accountable. Systems are going to change."

"I know."

"And your daughter—Maya—she's going to grow up in a world where—"

"I know," Sarah said, more sharply than she intended. "I know why I did it. You don't have to keep reminding me."

Morrison looked embarrassed.

"Sorry," he said. "I just wanted you to know that it matters. That you matter."

Sarah looked at her daughter.

"She matters," Sarah said quietly. "She's the only thing that matters."

The attack came at 2:17 AM.

Sarah woke to the sound of glass breaking—quiet, professional, the kind of breaking that suggested tools designed for exactly this purpose.

For a moment, she was frozen. The fear was total, absolute, the kind of fear that shut down everything else.

Then she heard Maya stir in the next room, and the fear became something else.

Something useful.

She moved before she was fully awake. Grabbed Maya from her bed. Ran for the panic room that the FBI had installed and made her practice finding in the dark.

"Mommy?" Maya's voice was small. Scared. "Mommy, what's happening?"

"It's okay, baby. It's okay. We're playing a game."

"I don't like this game."

"I know. I know. But we have to play it anyway."

The panic room was small—barely big enough for two people—but it had reinforced walls and a door that would take more than casual force to breach. Sarah pulled Maya inside, closed the door, and pressed the button that would send an alert to the

FBI.

Then she waited.

In the dark.

Holding her daughter.

Listening to the sounds of men moving through the apartment, searching, getting closer.

The FBI response time was supposed to be twelve minutes.

Justin and Erik arrived in seven.

They weren't supposed to be there. Weren't officially part of the operation. But Justin had been monitoring the safe house remotely—a habit he'd developed after David Chen, a paranoia that had saved lives more than once.

When the alarm triggered, he was already moving.

Erik was with him. Always was, for things like this.

They hit the building like a controlled explosion—fast, precise, devastating.

The men inside never knew what happened.

Sarah heard the gunfire first.

Four shots. Then three more. Then silence.

Then a knock on the panic room door.

"Mrs. Okonkwo?" A voice she didn't recognize. Calm. Professional. "It's safe to come out now."

She didn't move. Couldn't move. The fear had locked her in place, and no amount of calm professionalism was going to unlock it.

"Mommy?" Maya whispered. "Is the game over?"

"I don't know, baby. I don't know."

Another knock. Softer this time.

"Mrs. Okonkwo, my name is Justin. I work with the people protecting you. The men who came here tonight are… no longer a threat. But we need to move you somewhere safer, and we need to do it quickly."

Sarah's hand trembled on the door release.

"How do I know you're telling the truth?"

A pause. Then: "You don't. You have to decide whether to trust me. And I know that's hard, given what you've been through. But I

116

can tell you this: I could have left you in there. Let the FBI handle it when they arrived. Instead, I'm standing here, in the dark, asking for permission to help."

Sarah looked at Maya.

Maya looked back with eyes that were too young to hold this much fear.

Sarah opened the door.

The man on the other side was tall, well-dressed, with an expression that suggested he'd seen worse than this and expected to see worse again.

Behind him, another man—quieter, darker clothing, the kind of stillness that suggested coiled violence.

"I'm Justin," the first one said. "This is Erik. We're going to get you out of here."

"Where?"

"Somewhere the people who did this won't find you."

Sarah looked at the apartment beyond them. At the bodies on the floor. At the blood that was seeping into the carpet.

"They found us here," she said. "They found us in an FBI safe house."

Justin nodded slowly.

"Yes. They did."

"How?"

"That's what we're going to find out." He glanced at Erik, who was already scanning the room, looking for something. "But first, we get you safe. Really safe. The kind of safe that doesn't depend on systems that can be compromised."

Sarah held Maya tighter.

"Why should I trust you?"

Justin smiled. It was a tired smile. A sad smile. The smile of someone who had been asked this question before and knew there was no good answer.

"Because we're here," he said. "And we're not leaving until you're safe."

The new safe house wasn't a safe house at all.

It was a cabin in the mountains of Vermont—no connection to any database, no record in any system, purchased with cash thirty years ago by someone who no longer existed.

Erik had found it. Of course he had. Erik had safe houses scattered across three continents, each one invisible, each one waiting for exactly this kind of emergency.

Sarah and Maya arrived at dawn. The air was cold. The trees were thick. The world felt impossibly far away.

"How long?" Sarah asked.

Justin was standing on the porch, watching the road that didn't appear on any map.

"As long as it takes," he said.

"To do what?"

He turned to look at her.

"To make sure the people who came for you can never come for anyone again."

It took three weeks.

Three weeks of Sarah and Maya in the cabin, learning to breathe again, learning to sleep without waking at every sound.

Three weeks of Justin and Erik systematically dismantling the network that had tried to kill them.

Sarah didn't know the details. Didn't want to know. But she saw the news reports—the arrests, the resignations, the sudden "retirements" of executives who had seemed untouchable.

She saw the file she had created do what she had hoped it would do.

She saw justice.

Or something like it.

Justin came to the cabin one last time.

"It's over," he said. "The network is gone. The leak in the FBI has been identified and removed. You can go home."

Sarah was sitting on the porch, watching Maya play in the yard. The fear was still there—would probably always be there—but it was smaller now. Manageable.

"Thank you," she said.

Justin shook his head.

"You did the hard part. You saw something wrong and you reported it. That took courage."

"Courage almost got me killed."

"Yes. It did." He sat down beside her. "But it also exposed a fraud that was stealing from forty thousand people. Retirement funds. Pensions. Life savings. All of it would have been gone if you hadn't spoken up."

Sarah watched her daughter.

"I keep thinking about what would have happened," she said. "If you hadn't been there. If you hadn't arrived when you did."

"Don't."

"How can I not?"

Justin was quiet for a moment.

"I knew someone," he said. "An accountant. David Chen. He found evidence of fraud, just like you did. He reported it, just like you did."

"What happened to him?"

"We didn't get there in time."

Sarah closed her eyes.

"So I'm lucky."

"No." Justin's voice was firm. "You're alive because we learned from what happened to him. Because we started watching closer, moving faster, taking nothing for granted."

He looked at her.

"David Chen's death wasn't meaningless. It taught us to be better. And because of that, you're sitting here watching your daughter play."

Sarah wiped her eyes.

"That's supposed to make me feel better?"

"No. It's supposed to help you understand why we do what we do."

He stood.

"Go home, Mrs. Okonkwo. Live your life. Watch Maya grow up. And when she's old enough to understand, tell her what you did. Tell her that her mother saw something wrong and had the courage to fix it."

"And if she asks about the men who saved us?"

Justin smiled.

"Tell her we were just doing our job."

He walked to the car where Erik was waiting.

Sarah watched them go.

Three months later, Sarah Okonkwo received an anonymous letter.

Inside was a photograph of Maya, taken through the window of their new house, playing with the dog they'd gotten after returning from Vermont.

Below the photograph, in neat handwriting:

She's safe. She's happy. She's going to have a good life.

>

That's what you did.

>

That's what courage looks like.

Sarah cried for an hour.

Then she framed the photograph and put it on her desk, where she could see it every day.

A reminder of what she had done.

A reminder of what it had cost.

A reminder that somewhere out there, in the spaces between systems and protocols and official channels, there were people who stood on the line where responsibility stopped.

People who noticed.

People who cared.

People who, when it mattered most, arrived in time.

CHAPTER 16

The Different Call

The target was a pharmaceutical executive named Harrison Webb.

Not the CEO—Webb was smarter than that. He was the Chief Compliance Officer, the man whose job was to ensure that Meridian Pharmaceuticals followed every regulation, honored every ethical obligation, maintained every standard of corporate responsibility.

He was also the man who had designed the system that killed thirty-seven people.

The system was elegant, in a terrible way. Clinical trial data that was technically accurate but strategically incomplete. Risk assessments that highlighted minor concerns while burying major ones. A paper trail so meticulously constructed that any investigation would find exactly what Webb wanted them to find: evidence of good faith effort, reasonable precautions, unfortunate but unforeseeable outcomes.

Thirty-seven people dead from a drug that Webb knew was dangerous.

And not a single piece of evidence that would hold up in court.

"We go in hard," Justin said. "Same approach as Kozlov. Psychological pressure, escalating consequences, break him until he gives us something we can use."

They were in a safe house outside Philadelphia. Rachel had been with them for three weeks now—long enough to prove her analytical value, long enough to earn a seat at the table, not yet long enough to feel like she belonged there.

"That won't work," she said.

Justin looked at her. "It's worked before."

"On people who had something to lose. Webb doesn't." Rachel pulled up his file on her laptop. "He's divorced. No children. Parents deceased. No close friends that we've identified. His entire life is his work, and his work is untouchable because he's designed it that way."

"Everyone has something to lose."

"Not everyone. Some people have already lost everything that mattered and rebuilt themselves around the loss." Rachel met Justin's eyes. "You can't threaten a man who's already empty."

Erik, who had been silent, spoke. "What do you suggest?"

Rachel hesitated. This was the moment. The test she'd been waiting for without knowing she was waiting.

"We don't threaten him," she said. "We offer him something."

"Offer him what? Immunity? We can't—"

"Not immunity. Purpose." Rachel turned the laptop so they could see the screen. "Webb wasn't always like this. Fifteen years ago, he was a whistleblower. He exposed his previous employer for the same kind of fraud he's now committing. Cost him everything—his career, his marriage, his reputation."

"And then he became the thing he fought against."

"Because the system punished him for being right." Rachel's voice was quiet. "He tried to do the right thing, and it destroyed him. So he decided that if the system was broken, he might as well profit from the breakage."

"That's not an excuse."

"No. It's a vulnerability." Rachel leaned forward. "Webb doesn't believe anyone actually cares about doing the right thing. He thinks everyone is like him—idealists who eventually surrender to reality. If we show him that's not true…"

"He might remember who he used to be," Erik finished.

"Maybe. Or maybe he'll laugh in our faces and we'll have to do it Justin's way. But I think it's worth trying."

Justin took his time before answering.

"You want to appeal to his conscience."

"I want to appeal to his grief. For who he used to be."

"And if you're wrong?"

"Then I'm wrong, and we fall back to pressure tactics." Rachel held his gaze. "But I'm not wrong. I've studied this man for two weeks. I know his patterns, his history, his losses. I know what broke him."

"You think you can unbreak him?"

"I think I can remind him that he's broken. Sometimes that's enough."

Justin looked at Erik.

Erik's expression was unreadable—but then, Erik's expression was always unreadable.

"Let her try," Erik said.

Rachel met Webb alone.

Justin had argued against it. So had Erik, in his quiet way. But Rachel had insisted.

"He won't talk to you," she'd said. "You represent exactly what he expects—force, coercion, the same systems that crushed him before. He'll see you coming and shut down."

"And he won't see you coming?"

"He'll see a woman who reminds him of who he used to be. An analyst who asks questions. Someone who got fired for doing the right thing." Rachel smiled grimly. "Someone who should have learned her lesson by now."

The meeting was in a coffee shop in Center City. Public, neutral, the kind of place where violence was impractical and conversation was possible.

Webb arrived exactly on time. He was smaller than Rachel expected—slight, graying, with the hunched posture of someone who had spent decades trying to disappear into paperwork.

"Ms. Torres," he said, sitting down. "I assume you're not actually a journalist."

"No."

"And you're not from the FDA, or the DOJ, or any of the other agencies that have tried to build cases against Meridian."

"No."

"Then who are you?"

Rachel considered several answers. Chose the truth.

"I'm someone who got fired three times for doing what you used to do. For asking questions. For refusing to pretend that wrong things were right." She met his eyes. "I'm someone who could have become you."

Webb's expression flickered. Just for a moment.

"You don't know anything about me."

"I know you exposed ViralTech in 2009. I know it cost you everything. I know you spent two years unemployed, blacklisted, watching the people you'd exposed get promoted while you couldn't find work."

"Ancient history."

"I know you started at Meridian as a true believer. Thought you could change things from the inside. Thought you could be the good guy in a bad system."

"Naive."

"I know the exact moment you gave up." Rachel leaned forward. "December 14th, 2015. The internal memo about the Cardiox trial data. You flagged the problems. You documented the risks. You did everything right."

Webb's face had gone pale.

"And they ignored you," Rachel continued. "They buried your report and pushed the drug through anyway. And when people started dying, you realized that nothing you did would ever matter. That the system was designed to protect itself, not the people it was supposed to serve."

"Stop."

"So you stopped fighting. You stopped caring. You became the system, because if you couldn't beat it, at least you could profit from it."

"I said stop."

Rachel stopped.

The silence stretched between them. In the coffee shop, normal people had normal conversations, unaware that two people at a corner table were discussing thirty-seven deaths and the architecture of moral collapse.

"What do you want?" Webb asked finally. His voice was different now. Smaller.

"I want you to remember why you used to care."

"I don't care anymore. That's the point."

"I don't believe you." Rachel reached into her bag and pulled out a folder. "These are the families of the people who died from Cardiox. Not statistics. People. Maria Gonzalez, who was fifty-two and had three grandchildren. Thomas Park, who was training for a marathon. Jennifer Walsh, who had just gotten engaged."

She spread the photos across the table.

"You know their names," Rachel said softly. "I can see it in your face. You've memorized every single one."

Webb stared at the photos.

His hands were trembling.

"What happens if I talk?" he asked, twenty minutes later.

"You'll lose everything. Again. Career, reputation, whatever's left of your professional life."

"And in return?"

"In return, you get to be Harrison Webb again. The one who blew the whistle. The one who cared." Rachel gathered the photos. "You don't get to undo what you've done. But you get to stop doing it. And you get to help us make sure the people who built this system face consequences."

"Consequences." Webb laughed bitterly. "I've seen what consequences look like in this industry. Golden parachutes and early retirement."

"Not this time."

Something in Rachel's voice made him look up.

"Who are you people?"

"We're the line," Rachel said. "The place where responsibility stops being optional."

Webb stared at the table.

Then he asked for another coffee.

And started talking.

Afterward, Justin was waiting outside.

"You were right," he admitted.

"I know."

"He gave us everything. The internal communications, the suppressed studies, the names of everyone involved in the cover-up."

"I know."

"That's going to bring down half of Meridian's executive team."

"I know." Rachel allowed herself a small smile. "And nobody lost a toe."

Justin laughed—a genuine laugh, surprised out of him.

"Erik's way has its uses."

"So does mine." Rachel looked at him. "I'm not saying your methods are wrong. I'm saying they're not the only methods. Sometimes people need to be broken. And sometimes they need to be reminded that they don't have to stay broken."

"That's very philosophical."

"I'm an analyst. We overthink everything."

They walked toward the car where Erik was waiting.

"Rachel," Justin said.

"Yes?"

"Welcome to the team."

She didn't smile. But something loosened in her chest—a tension she'd been carrying for weeks. Months. Years.

"Thank you," she said.

And meant it.

Erik watched them approach the car.

He had seen the way Rachel Torres processed the operation—not with the numbness that came from shock, not with the excitement that came from adrenaline, but with the careful analysis that came from understanding. She was cataloguing. Learning. Adapting.

She'll be good at this, he thought. *Better than good.*

And then, unbidden: *Anna would have liked her.*

The thought came with the familiar ache—not sharp anymore, just present, the way scar tissue was present. He had learned to live with it. Had learned to use it. Every operation was partly for her now, whether he acknowledged it or not.

Rachel Torres had lost people too. He had read her file. He knew the particular geography of her grief.

Maybe that was why Justin had chosen her.

126

Or maybe Justin had simply seen what Erik was seeing now: someone who understood that the work wasn't about revenge, or redemption, or any of the things that burned out operatives in three years or less.

It was about the line.

It was always about the line.

CHAPTER 17

The Safe House

Every operative needs a place to disappear.

Justin and Erik had seventeen such locations scattered across four continents. The one in Prague was their favorite—a converted monastery purchased through shell companies, abandoned-looking from outside, a fortress within.

"We need to talk," Justin said.

They were in what had once been the chapel—now an operational planning center, walls lined with maps and intelligence.

Erik was cleaning a weapon. He found it meditative.

"About?"

"The network. The pattern Gerald identified."

"The financial flows."

"More than that." Justin walked to one of the maps. "Look at this. Every target we've hit in the past year. Every network we've dismantled."

Erik set down the weapon and joined him.

Red pins marked completed operations. Blue pins marked ongoing investigations. Yellow pins marked potential targets.

"What do you see?"

"A lot of red pins."

"What else?"

Erik studied the map.

"They're clustered. Not randomly distributed. There's a pattern."

"Exactly. We've been hitting targets in specific regions—Eastern Europe, Southeast Asia, parts of Africa. And we've been avoiding others."

"We go where the intelligence takes us."

"Do we?" Justin pointed to a section notably empty of pins. "Central America. South America. The Caribbean. Just as corrupt. But we haven't touched them."

"The intelligence hasn't pointed there."

"Because we've been following intelligence that someone else is providing." Justin's voice was quiet. "What if they've all been steering us?"

CHAPTER 18

The Witness

Marcus Webb had been watching Lampert and Block for three weeks.

Not officially, of course. Officially, Webb was a contractor—one of hundreds who moved through the intelligence community doing work that couldn't be attributed to any government. His official assignment was something involving signal analysis. His actual assignment was observation.

Someone wanted to understand how they worked.

Someone was willing to pay very well for that understanding.

Webb had taken the money without asking too many questions. Questions led to complications, and complications led to the kind of trouble that ended careers—or lives.

He was good at his job. Twenty years of surveillance work had taught him how to become invisible, how to blend into backgrounds, how to be a face that people looked through without seeing.

It worked on most people.

It didn't work on them.

He realized they knew on day four.

Nothing obvious. No confrontation, no acknowledgment. Just a small adjustment in their routine—a different café, a different route, a different pattern that somehow always kept him exactly where they wanted him.

They were watching him watch them.

And they were doing it without revealing that they knew.

Webb had been in the surveillance game for two decades. He had followed drug dealers and diplomats, terrorists and businessmen. He had never encountered anyone who could turn the observation around so completely, so effortlessly.

It was humbling.

It was also terrifying.

The meeting happened in Prague.

Webb was sitting at a café—his usual cover, a businessman traveling through, nothing remarkable—when Justin Lampert sat down across from him.

"You're good," Lampert said. "Better than most. But you've been pacing us since Vienna, and it's starting to get awkward."

Webb considered his options. He had a weapon—everyone in his line of work carried something—but he had also read the files. He knew what Lampert and Block were capable of. Reaching for that weapon would be the last thing he ever did.

"I don't know what you're talking about," he said. Professional denial. Standard procedure.

"Sure you do." Lampert ordered coffee from the waitress, completely at ease. "The question is: do we make this difficult, or do we have an actual conversation?"

Webb studied him.

There was something in Lampert's eyes—not quite humor, not quite threat, but something in between. An invitation, perhaps. Or a test.

"An actual conversation," Webb said finally.

Lampert smiled.

"Good choice."

The conversation lasted three hours.

Lampert talked. Block—who had appeared from somewhere Webb hadn't been watching, which was impossible because Webb had been watching everywhere—listened. And Webb learned more about the two men he'd been assigned to observe than three weeks of surveillance had revealed.

"You want to know our methodology," Lampert said. "Fair enough. Here it is: we don't have one."

"Everyone has a methodology."

"No. Everyone has patterns. Habits. Things they do because they've always done them." Lampert leaned forward. "We have principles. That's different."

"What principles?"

Block spoke for the first time. His voice was quiet, measured, a voice that made you lean in to hear it.

131

"The line," he said.

"What line?"

"The line where responsibility stops." Block's eyes were calm but intense. "Everyone draws it somewhere. Most people draw it close—their family, their friends, maybe their neighborhood. They tell themselves that anything beyond that line isn't their problem."

"And you?"

"We draw it further out," Lampert said. "Further than most people think is reasonable. Further than most people think is sane."

"Why?"

Lampert and Block exchanged a look. Something passed between them—not words, just understanding.

"Because someone has to," Lampert said. "Because if we don't, then the people who cross the line—the ones who hurt people, who exploit systems, who think they're untouchable—they win. Every time. And we're not okay with that."

Webb's jaw tightened.

"That sounds exhausting."

"It is."

"And dangerous."

"Also yes."

"So why do you keep doing it?"

Lampert finished his coffee.

"Because every time we don't," he said, "someone suffers. Someone loses their family. Someone dies for doing the right thing. Someone, somewhere, pays the price because we decided it wasn't our problem."

He stood.

"Go back to your handlers," he said. "Tell them what you saw. Tell them we knew you were watching, and we let you watch anyway. Tell them that if they want to understand us, they should stop trying to analyze us and start trying to help."

"Help with what?"

Lampert smiled.

"We'll send them a list."

Webb filed his report three days later.

It was sixty-two pages long—the most thorough assessment he'd ever written. It covered their movements, their methods, their apparent capabilities.

But the part that his handlers found most interesting was his conclusion:

ASSESSMENT: Subjects Lampert and Block operate outside conventional parameters. They do not follow standard protocols, do not respect jurisdictional boundaries, and do not respond to traditional forms of pressure or incentive.

>

However, their effectiveness is undeniable. In the three weeks of observation, they resolved four situations that official channels had been unable to address—including the complete dismantling of a trafficking network operating across three countries.

>

RECOMMENDATION: Do not attempt to control, contain, or eliminate these subjects. Instead, consider them a resource. Provide them with intelligence. Remove bureaucratic obstacles. Let them work.

>

The alternative—treating them as threats—would be both dangerous and wasteful. They are not our enemies. They are, in their own way, working toward the same goals we are.

>

They are simply better at it.

The report was classified immediately.

Webb never learned what happened to it—whether it was filed, discussed, acted upon, or simply buried in the endless bureaucracy of intelligence work.

But he noticed something in the months that followed.

The interference that had plagued Lampert and Block's operations began to disappear. Safe houses that had been compromised became available again. Contacts who had stopped responding started responding again.

Someone, somewhere, had listened.

Someone had decided that maybe—just maybe—it was better to have them as allies than enemies.

Webb kept watching. Not officially—he had other assignments now—but he tracked their work when he could.

And every time he saw a report of something impossible being accomplished—a network dismantled, a witness saved, a line held—he smiled.

He knew who was responsible.

Even if no one else ever would.

Years later, Webb told the story to a young analyst who asked about his career.

"I watched the best in the world," he said. "For three weeks, I had a front-row seat to something that shouldn't exist."

"What shouldn't exist?"

"Two men who believe in something bigger than themselves. Two men who hold a line that everyone else has abandoned."

He paused.

"You want to know the truth about Lampert and Block? The truth is that they're exactly what they appear to be. No hidden agenda. No secret motivation. They do what they do because they believe it's right."

"That's hard to accept."

"I know." Webb smiled tiredly. "In our world, everyone has an angle. Everyone is working toward something personal. The idea that someone might actually be doing it for the right reasons—that's hard to believe."

"But you believe it."

"I do." Webb nodded. "I watched them for three weeks. I saw how they worked. I saw the choices they made when they thought no one was watching."

He stood.

"They're the real thing, kid. And if you're smart, you'll stay out of their way and let them work."

"And if I'm not smart?"

Webb laughed.

"Then you'll learn the same lesson everyone else learns," he said. "The hard way."

He walked out of the room, leaving the young analyst to wonder what, exactly, he had meant.

And whether there was any chance of being on the right side of whatever was coming.

Erik knew, before Justin said a word, that they were going to disagree.

He could feel it building—the tension that came from different conclusions drawn from the same facts. They had worked together long enough that disagreement had its own texture, its own weight. Like pressure changes before a storm.

Petrov has to die.

The thought wasn't emotional. It was mathematical. Petrov had crossed a line that couldn't be uncrossed. The evidence was clear. The pattern was undeniable. Allowing him to live would send a message that some things were tolerable.

Some things were not tolerable.

But Justin would see it differently. Justin always looked for the angle, the approach, the possibility that violence wasn't the only answer. It was one of the things Erik respected about him—and one of the things that occasionally drove him to silent fury.

Tonight would be one of those nights.

Erik prepared himself for the argument he knew was coming.

CHAPTER 19

The Disagreement

The argument started at 2 AM, in a safe house that smelled like old coffee and older secrets.

"He has to die," Erik said.

Justin stopped pacing. Turned to look at his partner of seven years.

"No."

"He's killed eleven people, Justin. Eleven that we know of. The trafficking network he runs has destroyed hundreds of lives. He's not going to stop."

"He might. With the right pressure—"

"There is no pressure that changes what he is." Erik's voice was flat. Certain. "Viktor Petrov is a predator. You don't rehabilitate predators. You remove them."

Justin felt the familiar weight of this conversation—the one they'd been avoiding for years. The line between them that they'd pretended didn't exist.

"That's not our call to make."

"Then whose call is it?" Erik stood, moved to the window, looked out at a city full of people who would never know this conversation was happening. "The authorities won't touch him. He has connections in three governments. His lawyers have buried every investigation. The system you believe in has failed, completely and thoroughly."

"The system isn't the only option."

"No. We're the option. And our option is permanent removal."

"Our option is consequences. Not executions."

Erik turned. His face was calm, but something moved behind his eyes—something old and cold and patient.

"What's the difference?"

Justin had known this moment would come.

He'd known it since the beginning, really. Since the first time he'd seen Erik work—the precision, the efficiency, the utter lack of hesitation. Erik Block was a weapon that had learned to aim itself. And weapons, eventually, wanted to be used.

"The difference," Justin said carefully, "is choice. Petrov can choose to cooperate. To give us information. To help us dismantle his network instead of just cutting off the head and watching another one grow."

"And if he doesn't choose that?"

"Then we escalate. Pressure. Leverage. The things we've always done."

"Until when? Until he escapes? Until he kills someone else? Until the next Viktor Petrov emerges from the wreckage and we start the whole process over?"

Erik's voice hadn't risen, but the intensity behind it was unmistakable.

"I'm tired, Justin. I'm tired of half-measures. I'm tired of letting monsters walk away because we're afraid of becoming monsters ourselves."

"That fear is what keeps us human."

"That fear is what keeps them alive." Erik stepped closer. "Anna is dead because I was afraid. Because I hesitated. Because I believed—like you believe—that there was always another way."

The name hung in the air between them.

Justin had never heard Erik say it. Not like that. Not as a weapon.

"That's not fair."

"Nothing is fair. That's the point." Erik's voice softened, but didn't warm. "I loved her, Justin. I loved her more than I've ever loved anything. And she died because I tried to do this your way. I tried to believe in rehabilitation, in consequences, in the possibility that people could change."

"Some people can."

"Not all people. Not Petrov." Erik met his eyes. "I know what I'm asking. I know what it costs. But I'm asking anyway: let me do what needs to be done."

The silence stretched.

Justin thought about every operation they'd run together. Every line they'd held. Every moment when the easy answer was violence and they'd chosen something harder.

He thought about who they'd become. Who they were still becoming.

And he thought about Viktor Petrov. The eleven confirmed kills. The hundreds of victims. The network that would survive any arrest, any prosecution, any consequence short of absolute termination.

"No," he said finally.

Erik's expression didn't change.

"Then we have a problem."

"We have a disagreement. It's not the same thing."

"It's not?"

"No." Justin sat down heavily. "A problem means we can't work together. A disagreement means we work together anyway, even though we don't agree."

"How does that work?"

"I don't know. We figure it out." Justin looked up at his partner. "I'm not saying you're wrong, Erik. I'm saying I can't let you do this. Not because Petrov deserves to live—he doesn't. But because if we start deciding who lives and dies based on our judgment alone, we become something else. Something I'm not willing to become."

"Even if it means more people die?"

"Even then." The words hurt to say. "Because the moment we lose the line between us and them, we lose everything. We become just another force in the world, doing violence for reasons that feel right to us. And that's exactly what they do. That's exactly what we're fighting against."

Erik let the silence stretch.

"You're asking me to watch him walk away."

"I'm asking you to trust that there's another path. And if there isn't—if I'm wrong—then we revisit this conversation. But not tonight. Not like this."

They didn't resolve it.

That was the truth that neither of them wanted to admit: some disagreements couldn't be resolved. They could only be lived with, worked around, carried forward into operations that required absolute trust between people who didn't entirely agree.

"The Kiev operation," Erik said finally. "We proceed as planned?"

"As planned. Petrov gets the standard approach. Pressure, leverage, consequences."

"And if he doesn't break?"

Justin hesitated.

"Then we escalate."

"To what?"

"I don't know yet." Justin stood. Extended his hand. "But we figure it out together. That's the deal. That's how this works."

Erik looked at the hand.

For a moment—just a moment—Justin thought he might not take it.

Then Erik clasped his hand firmly.

"Together," he agreed.

It wasn't resolution. It wasn't peace.

But it was enough to keep going.

Three months later, Viktor Petrov would die in police custody.

Heart attack, the official report said. Natural causes.

Justin never asked Erik what really happened.

He told himself it was trust. That after seven years, he owed Erik the benefit of his silence. That partners didn't interrogate each other's methods.

But late at night, when the work was quiet and there was nothing to do but think, Justin wondered if silence was its own kind of crossing. If not asking was the same as approving. If the line he'd spent his career holding had shifted underneath him while he wasn't paying attention.

Some questions were better left unasked.

Some lines were better left unexamined.

And some disagreements never really ended—they just found new shapes to wear.

Justin carried that shape with him. It was heavier than he'd expected.

PART THREE

The Test

"Testing reveals character. Testing under pressure reveals truth."

— Dr. Alaric Voss, private journal

"They think they're testing us. They don't realize we've been testing them too."

— Justin Lampert, operational note

CHAPTER 20

The Man Who Reads the Reports

Gerald Morrison had been reading reports for twenty-three years.

Not just any reports. The kind of reports that didn't officially exist—the ones that came through channels without names, from operations without records, about people who did things that couldn't be discussed in polite company or impolite company or any company at all.

He had a system.

The system involved a filing cabinet (mental), a categorization protocol (arbitrary but consistent), and a small brown cat named Theodore who sat on his desk while he worked and judged him silently.

Theodore was seven years old and had never forgiven Gerald for the move from Maryland.

"You don't understand bureaucracy," Gerald told the cat, not for the first time. "In bureaucracy, you go where the reports go. And the reports went to Virginia."

Gerald returned to the file in front of him.

SUBJECTS: LAMPERT, JUSTIN / BLOCK, ERIK
CLASSIFICATION: EXHAUSTING

He'd been reading their reports for three years now. Three years of operations that defied categorization, of outcomes that shouldn't have been possible, of methodology that the Ethics Committee had given up trying to understand.

Three years of footnotes that made him question his career choices.

NOTE: Subject Lampert was asked why he approached the target through the kitchen entrance rather than the main door. His response: "The main door had a rug, and I didn't want to track in mud." When asked to clarify, he stated: "I'm not an animal, Gerald."

>

Subject Lampert has never met this analyst and should not know his name.

Gerald stared at that last line for a long time.

Theodore yawned.

The thing about Lampert and Block was that they weren't supposed to work.

Gerald had studied psychology. Had taken courses in behavioral analysis. Had read every paper on operational methodology that the Agency had ever produced.

None of it applied.

Two-person teams were inherently unstable. The dynamics were wrong—power imbalances, communication breakdowns, the inevitable friction of two personalities in high-stress situations. Every study showed that optimal team size was four to six, with clear hierarchies and defined roles.

Lampert and Block had no hierarchy. No defined roles. No clear methodology.

They just… worked.

Gerald had a theory about this. He'd never written it down—writing things down made them official, and official things got read by people with opinions—but he thought about it often.

His theory was that Lampert and Block succeeded because they didn't care about succeeding.

Not in the way that other operatives cared. They didn't track their statistics. Didn't compare themselves to their peers. Didn't seem to notice or care whether anyone was watching, evaluating, judging.

They just did what they did, and what they did happened to be effective.

It was infuriating.

It was also, Gerald had to admit, kind of inspiring.

The latest report was from an operation in Morocco.

A desalination plant. A saboteur. Fifty thousand people who depended on clean water.

Lampert and Block had resolved the situation in seventeen hours—not through the methodical approach that the analysts had recommended, not through the coordination with local authorities that protocol required, but through what the report described as "aggressive improvisation."

Gerald read the details.

He read them again.

He made a note in the margin: *How?*

Then he crossed it out, because he knew he would never get an answer.

There was a knock on his door.

"Come in," Gerald said, not looking up.

The door opened. A woman entered—young, ambitious, the kind of analyst who still believed that understanding the system meant controlling it.

"Mr. Morrison? I have a question about the Lampert/Block files."

Gerald sighed. "Everyone has questions about the Lampert/Block files. The files don't have answers."

"But there must be some pattern—"

"There is no pattern." Gerald finally looked up. "There is no methodology. There is no system that can be documented, replicated, or taught."

"Then how do they do it?"

Gerald considered the question.

He thought about the reports he'd read. The operations that shouldn't have succeeded. The outcomes that defied explanation.

He thought about two men who had, somehow, found each other in a world designed to keep people apart.

"They believe," Gerald said finally.

"In what?"

"In the line." He gestured at the files on his desk—three years of documentation, of evidence, of attempts to understand something that resisted understanding. "They believe there's a line. A boundary between acceptable and unacceptable. Between the things we allow and the things we shouldn't."

"That's... vague."

"Yes. It is." Gerald smiled tiredly. "But vague doesn't mean meaningless. And somewhere in that vagueness, they found something that works. Something that lets them do the impossible, over and over, without burning out or breaking down."

He returned to his report.

"I've been reading about them for three years," he said. "And I still don't understand how they do what they do. But I understand why."

"Why?"

"Because someone has to." Gerald's voice was quiet. "Because the line exists, whether we acknowledge it or not. And because they decided—both of them, somehow, separately and together—that standing on that line was worth the cost."

The young analyst was silent for a moment.

"That sounds lonely," she said finally.

Gerald thought about this.

"It probably is," he agreed. "But I don't think they notice. They have each other."

He made another note in the margin.

Ongoing.

That was all he could say. That was all anyone could say.

Lampert and Block were ongoing.

And Gerald Morrison would keep reading their reports until one of them stopped being written.

He hoped that day was very far away.

Gerald scratched behind his ears and returned to work.

CHAPTER 21

What Erik Wants

They were in a safe house in Prague when Erik said something he had never said before.

"I want to stop."

Justin looked up from the files he was reviewing. For a moment, he thought he'd misheard.

"What?"

"I want to stop." Erik was standing at the window, looking out at a city he had killed people in, years ago, for reasons that had seemed clear at the time. "Not today. Not tomorrow. But eventually. I want to know that there's an end to this."

Justin set down the files.

In seven years of partnership, Erik had never expressed doubt. Never questioned the work. Never suggested that there was any future beyond the next operation, the next target, the next line to hold.

"What brought this on?"

"Rachel."

"Rachel?"

"She has a life. Outside of this." Erik turned from the window. "I watched her on the Webb operation. After it was done—after we had what we needed—she went home. To an apartment with books and plants and a cat that someone feeds when she's traveling."

"You have a cat. Theodore."

"Theodore is Gerald's cat. I borrowed him because Gerald was worried about surveillance." Erik's expression didn't change, but something shifted behind his eyes. "Rachel has a life, Justin. A real one. With things in it that aren't about the work."

"And you don't."

"I don't know what I have." Erik sat down across from him. "For years, that was fine. After Anna... I didn't want a life. I wanted revenge, and then I wanted purpose, and the work provided both. But revenge is over. The people who killed her are dead. And

146

purpose..."

He trailed off.

"Purpose isn't enough?" Justin asked.

"Purpose is exactly enough. That's the problem." Erik leaned forward. "I'm good at this, Justin. We're good at this. We could do it forever—find targets, hold lines, maintain consequences. We could do it until we're too old or too slow, and then someone would replace us, and the work would continue."

"That sounds like success."

"It sounds like existence. Not the same thing."

Justin took his time before answering.

He understood what Erik was saying. Had felt echoes of it himself, in the moments between operations when the adrenaline faded and the weight of what they did settled back into place.

"What would you want?" he asked finally. "If you could have anything. If this could end."

Erik considered the question seriously. It deserved serious consideration.

"I would want what Anna wanted for me," he said. "A life where the work was done. Where the lines didn't need holding because they had been established, accepted, enforced by systems that actually functioned."

"That world doesn't exist."

"I know. But I would want to believe it could." Erik's voice was quiet. "I would want to believe that everything we've done—the violence, the sacrifices, the parts of ourselves we've lost—that it was building toward something. Not just maintaining. Building."

"You think we're only maintaining?"

"I think we're holding ground. Important ground. But holding isn't advancing. And eventually, holding becomes all you know how to do."

Justin thought about this.

"Is this why you pushed back on the Petrov approach?"

"Partly. I pushed back because I was tired of half-measures. But underneath that..." Erik paused. "Underneath that, I think I was angry. Angry at myself for still believing that there's a version of this where we win. Where we don't just survive the work—we complete it."

"And killing Petrov felt like completion."

"It felt like control. Which isn't the same thing, but in the moment, they feel similar."

The safe house was quiet.

Outside, Prague went about its business—tourists and locals and ordinary people living ordinary lives, unaware that two men in an unremarkable apartment were discussing whether it was possible to want something beyond the violence that defined them.

"I don't know if we can stop," Justin admitted. "I don't know if I know how to be anything else."

"I know. Neither do I." Erik almost smiled—one of his rare, fleeting expressions that appeared and vanished before you could fully register it. "But I want to learn. Someday. I want to believe that there's a version of the future where Erik Block is something other than a weapon."

"What would that look like?"

"I don't know. Something quiet. Something with books and plants and a cat that's actually mine." Erik looked at him. "Something where I remember what Anna saw in me. Something worth the years she spent believing I could be more."

Justin felt something shift in his chest.

"She was right about you," he said. "Anna. Whatever she saw—she was right."

"How do you know?"

"Because you're sitting here asking these questions. Because you want something beyond the work. Because after everything you've done, everything you've lost, you're still hoping."

Justin leaned forward.

"That's not weakness, Erik. That's the whole point. That's what separates us from the people we fight against—they've stopped hoping. They've accepted that the world is dark and cruel, and they've made themselves comfortable in the darkness."

"And we haven't?"

"We've made ourselves effective in the darkness. That's different." Justin smiled. "We still believe in the light. Even when we can't see it. Even when it seems impossible. We still believe it's out there somewhere."

Erik let the silence stretch.

"Anna said something similar," he said finally. "The night before Prague. She said that the only way to survive the work was to remember why you started doing it."

"Why did you start?"

"Because someone had to hold the line. Because I had the skills to do it. Because after she died, it was the only thing that made sense."

"And now?"

Erik looked at him.

"Now I do it because it's what I do. Because it's who I am. Because every time I think about stopping, I think about all the lines that would go unheld, all the consequences that would go unenforced."

"But you still want to stop."

"Someday. Yes." Erik stood. Moved back to the window. "Someday I want to stop. I want to know what it feels like to be a person again. To have a life that isn't defined by the work."

"Then that's what we'll work toward," Justin said. "Not today. Not tomorrow. But as a goal. As something we're building toward."

"You think that's possible?"

"I think everything worth having seems impossible until someone makes it possible." Justin joined him at the window. "We've done impossible things before. We'll do them again."

They stood together, looking out at a city that didn't know they existed, thinking about a future they could barely imagine.

"Thank you," Erik said quietly.

"For what?"

"For listening. For not telling me I'm weak for wanting something beyond this."

"You're the opposite of weak." Justin put a hand on his partner's shoulder. "You're the strongest person I know. And part of that strength is knowing what you want, even when you can't have it yet."

Erik didn't respond.

But something in his posture eased. Something that had been coiled tight for years relaxed, just slightly.

It wasn't resolution.

But it was acknowledgment.

And sometimes, that was the first step toward something better.

CHAPTER 22

Professional Curiosity

Three months before the Morocco test.

Three months before the systematic campaign to understand Lampert and Block.

Three months before everything changed.

Dr. Alaric Voss sat in his office, surrounded by files he shouldn't have, studying patterns he shouldn't see.

The room was dark except for the glow of multiple screens, each one displaying a different piece of the puzzle he had been assembling for two years. Incident reports. Financial traces. Satellite imagery. The accumulated detritus of two men who left chaos in their wake and answers in their absence.

SUBJECT: Lampert, Justin

SUBJECT: Block, Erik

CLASSIFICATION: Ongoing

The files had grown thick. Thousands of pages. Hundreds of operations. A catalogue of impossibilities that defied every model Voss had built.

He took a sip of cold coffee and continued reading.

The first file was from Prague, six years ago.

A trafficking network that had operated for a decade, moving human cargo across borders with impunity. Local authorities had been compromised. International cooperation had stalled. The network had become, for all practical purposes, invisible.

Lampert and Block had dismantled it in nine days.

Voss studied the timeline. The precision of it. The way they had moved from target to target, never rushing, never making mistakes, always one step ahead of the response.

The official report attributed their success to "superior intelligence gathering and tactical execution."

Voss knew that was incomplete.

What the report didn't capture was the why. The motivation. The principle that drove two men to spend nine days dismantling an operation that had nothing to do with them, that paid them nothing, that offered no reward except the knowledge that it was done.

That was the part Voss couldn't model.

That was the part that kept him awake.

The second file was from Berlin, four years ago.

A financial scheme that had been siphoning money from pension funds—small amounts, carefully hidden, accumulating into millions over time. The people responsible were protected by layers of lawyers, shell companies, and the general assumption that white-collar crime was victimless.

Lampert and Block had proven otherwise.

Twelve arrests. Complete asset recovery. A system that had seemed impenetrable, reduced to rubble in three weeks.

But what fascinated Voss wasn't the result.

It was the method.

They hadn't gone after the principals first. They had started at the edges—the accountants, the middlemen, the small players who thought they were too insignificant to notice. One by one, they had turned them. Flipped them. Made them understand that cooperation was in their best interest.

By the time they reached the top, there was nothing left to defend.

"Elegant," Voss murmured to himself. "Systematic. Almost beautiful."

He made a note: *They understand pressure points. They know how systems fail.*

The third file was from Istanbul, two years ago.

This one was different.

A diplomat's daughter had been kidnapped. Standard ransom situation—pay the money, get the girl back, pretend it never happened. The family had been prepared to pay. The government had been prepared to look the other way.

Lampert and Block had not been prepared to accept that.

They had found the kidnappers in forty-eight hours. They had extracted the girl without paying a cent. They had left behind a message—a message that spread through the criminal underworld with the speed of bad news and the weight of consequence.

This is not acceptable. This will not be tolerated. Touch one more child, and we will find you.

Voss had interviewed three of the survivors—former kidnappers who had abandoned the profession after Istanbul. All of them had said the same thing:

"They weren't angry. They weren't emotional. They were just... certain. Absolutely certain that what they were doing was right. And that certainty—"

One of them had started crying at that point.

"That certainty was worse than anything else. Because you knew they meant it. You knew they would never stop."

Voss closed the files.

Two years. Models, simulations, consultants. And still, they eluded him.

Not their actions—but their motivation. That remained mysterious.

His phone buzzed. A message from one of his operatives.

New development. Morocco. Infrastructure crisis.

Voss read the details.

A water treatment plant serving fifty thousand people was failing. The official diagnosis was equipment malfunction, but Voss's sources suggested otherwise. Someone had sabotaged the plant—deliberately, systematically, with the skill of a professional.

He leaned back in his chair.

Opportunities like this didn't come often. A crisis that would draw Lampert and Block's attention. A chance to observe them in action, to study their methodology firsthand.

But there was a risk.

If they realized they were being watched—if they understood that the crisis had been manufactured—they would disappear. They would change their patterns, abandon their routines, become even more difficult to track.

Voss considered the variables.

He considered the potential reward.

He made his decision.

MEMO (PRIVATE)

SUBJECT: Operation Observation—Phase One

Date: [REDACTED]

The Morocco situation presents an ideal opportunity for controlled observation of Subjects Lampert and Block.

Recommended approach:

1. Allow crisis to develop naturally. Do not accelerate or interfere.

>

2. Deploy observation assets at key points. Maintain distance. Prioritize invisibility over coverage.

>

3. Document everything. Response time. Decision-making process. Communication patterns. Resource allocation.

>

4. Do not engage. Do not interact. Do not reveal presence under any circumstances.

Goal: Understand their methodology well enough to predict their behavior.

If we can predict their behavior, we can influence their actions.

If we can influence their actions, we can direct their capabilities toward more productive ends.

They are too valuable to eliminate.

They are too dangerous to ignore.

The only remaining option is understanding.

Voss sent the memo to himself. A record. A reminder of what he was trying to accomplish.

He returned to the files.

Somewhere in these thousands of pages, there had to be an answer. A pattern he had missed. A principle he hadn't identified.

He would find it.

He had to.

Because men like Lampert and Block didn't fit into the systems Voss understood. They operated outside the incentive structures that governed everyone else. They made choices that defied rational analysis.

And that made them unpredictable.

And unpredictable, in Voss's world, was unacceptable.

Outside his window, the city hummed with the activity of millions of people living their lives, making choices, following patterns they didn't even recognize.

Voss understood those patterns.

He had built his career on understanding them.

But Lampert and Block were different.

They had found something—some principle, some conviction, some line—that freed them from the patterns that bound everyone else.

Voss wanted that understanding.

Wanted it more than he had wanted anything in years.

And he was willing to wait as long as necessary to get it.

The Morocco test would be the first step.

There would be others.

And eventually, one way or another, he would understand.

He would understand, or he would destroy them trying.

Either outcome was acceptable.

The uncertainty was not.

CHAPTER 23

The Analyst

Gerald Morrison had a routine.

Every morning: 5:47 AM, eight-minute shower, one of seven identical gray suits, two eggs with toast, black coffee with two sugars. Then the drive to a building that didn't officially exist, to an office that contained a desk, a computer, a filing cabinet, and Theodore.

Theodore was a brown tabby cat who had appeared three years ago and refused to leave. No one knew how he'd gotten clearance for a secure government facility. Everyone had decided to stop asking.

"Good morning," Gerald said to Theodore.

Theodore regarded him with profound indifference.

Gerald sat down and began to work.

The work was reading. Thousands of documents per week. Over twenty-three years, he had read more classified material than probably any other person alive.

And he remembered all of it.

The Lampert-Block files were his current obsession. Every operation, every outcome, every Ethics Committee complaint. He had built a picture of two men more complete than any official assessment.

And he still didn't understand them.

"Why do they do it?" he asked Theodore.

Theodore yawned.

The pattern had started to take shape three months ago.

At first, it looked random—operations across different countries, different targets. A trafficking network in Prague. Money laundering in Cyprus. An arms dealer in Hamburg.

But Gerald had been reading files for twenty-three years. Coincidence was usually just a pattern you hadn't identified yet.

The connection was financial.

Every target was connected to the same money. Different shell companies, different jurisdictions—but underneath, the same source. Someone had built an empire. A network of networks.

And Lampert and Block were taking it apart, piece by piece.

"I see it too," Gerald said quietly. "I've seen it for months. I've written 2,847 memos. Seven have been read. None have resulted in action."

He looked at the files.

"But they act. They see a problem and they fix it. They don't wait for permission."

Gerald made his decision.

There was something else in the files.

Gerald almost missed it—a cross-reference buried in a footnote. A requisition form for "specialized interrogation equipment," filed three years ago, approved by an office that didn't appear on any organizational chart.

He pulled the thread.

The requisition led to a transfer authorization. The authorization led to a shipping manifest. The manifest led to—

Gerald stopped.

ASSET CLASSIFICATION: ANOMALOUS

PROJECT DESIGNATION: THRESHOLD

CLEARANCE REQUIRED: [REDACTED]

NOTE: Asset demonstrates properties inconsistent with known physical parameters. Recommend extreme caution in deployment.

"Theodore," Gerald said slowly, "what the hell is this?"

He had seen a lot of classified material in twenty-three years. Weapons programs. Biological research. The kind of things governments did in the dark.

But he had never seen anything classified as "anomalous."

He cross-referenced the project designation against Lampert and Block's operational history. Found a single match: an interrogation six months ago. A subject resistant to conventional methods. A note that said only: *THRESHOLD ASSET*

DEPLOYED. SUBJECT COOPERATIVE WITHIN FOUR MINUTES.

Four minutes.

The fastest conventional break Gerald had ever seen was six hours. Four minutes wasn't interrogation.

Four minutes was something else entirely.

He saved the files. Encrypted them. Added them to the package for Lampert and Block.

Someday, he promised himself, he would ask what was behind that door.

The message arrived in Justin Lampert's inbox at 3:47 AM, routed through seventeen servers.

You're missing pieces. I have them.

The network is bigger than you know. Meet me at the location in the attachment.

One condition: the source stays protected. I have twenty-three years of service and a cat who depends on me.

— G.M.

Justin woke Erik.

"We have a new player. Someone inside the system who says they want to help."

Erik read the message.

"Gerald Morrison," he said.

CHAPTER 24

The Journalist

Her name was Elena Vasquez, and she had been chasing this story for three years.

Three years of dead ends. Three years of sources who disappeared or recanted. Three years of editors who told her the story was too dangerous, too complicated, too likely to result in lawsuits that the paper couldn't afford.

But Elena was stubborn.

Stubborn was how you survived in investigative journalism. Stubborn was how you kept going when every rational part of your brain was screaming that you should stop.

And now, finally, she had something.

The documents had arrived in a manila envelope, left on her desk with no return address.

Financial records. Transaction logs. The kind of paper trail that connected the dots between legitimate businesses and criminal enterprises—the evidence that corporate lawyers spent millions of dollars trying to hide.

Elena read them three times.

Then she called her editor.

"I need protection," she said. "And a lawyer. And probably a bodyguard."

"That bad?"

"That good. This is the story, Mike. The one we've been chasing. The one that proves everything we suspected about Voss and his network."

Silence on the line.

"Where did you get the documents?"

"Anonymous source."

"Elena—"

"I know. I know it could be a setup. I know someone could be playing me. But the documents are real. I've verified them against three independent sources."

"How much time do you need?"

"Two weeks. Maybe three. I need to confirm everything, build the narrative, make it bulletproof."

"You have one week. After that, either we publish or we kill it."

Elena hung up.

One week to change everything.

She didn't know that she was being watched.

Not by the people she was investigating—they would come later. But by Gerald Morrison, who had been monitoring her work for six months.

Gerald had chosen Elena carefully.

She had a reputation for accuracy. She never published anything she couldn't prove. She protected her sources with a ferocity that had landed her in contempt of court twice and made her a hero among other journalists.

She was, in Gerald's assessment, exactly the right person to receive the documents.

The first threat came on day two.

A phone call in the middle of the night. A voice that was distorted but clearly hostile.

"Stop digging. Or we'll bury you."

Elena recorded the call. Analyzed it. Tried to trace it.

Dead end.

But the threat told her something important: she was on the right track. People didn't threaten journalists who were chasing nothing.

On day four, her apartment was broken into.

Nothing was taken—that wasn't the point. The point was the message: we know where you live. We can reach you whenever we want. We are watching.

Elena moved to a hotel. Then another hotel. She started varying her routes, her routines, her patterns.

She kept working.

Justin and Erik found her on day six.

She was in a coffee shop in Brooklyn, surrounded by documents, looking like she hadn't slept in days.

"Ms. Vasquez," Justin said, sitting down across from her. "We need to talk."

Elena's hand moved toward her bag—toward the mace she had started carrying after the break-in.

"I wouldn't," Erik said quietly, appearing at her side. "We're not here to hurt you. We're here to help."

Elena studied them.

She had been a journalist for fifteen years. She had interviewed murderers, politicians, and CEOs. She could read people.

These two were dangerous. But not to her.

"Who are you?"

"We're the people who sent you the documents."

Elena's eyes widened.

"You're—"

"Anonymous sources. Yes." Justin smiled. "We thought it was time to become slightly less anonymous."

The conversation lasted two hours.

Justin explained who they were. What they did. Why they had chosen Elena.

"The story you're writing," he said. "It's good. It's accurate. It will do real damage to Voss's network."

"But?"

"But publication won't be enough. Voss has lawyers who can tie up any legal proceedings for years. He has connections who can make investigations disappear. He has resources that most journalists can't imagine."

"So what do you want me to do?"

"Keep writing. Keep investigating. Build the most comprehensive, bulletproof story you possibly can." Justin leaned forward. "And then, when you're ready to publish, coordinate with us. We'll time our operational moves to coincide with your publication. Maximum impact. Maximum damage."

Elena thought about this.

"You want to use my story as cover for whatever you're planning."

"We want to use your story as part of a larger strategy. You expose the financial connections. We hit the operational infrastructure. Together, we take down something that neither of us could take down alone."

"Why should I trust you?"

Justin considered the question.

"You shouldn't," he admitted. "Not completely. But you should consider the alternative: you publish alone, Voss's lawyers bury you in litigation, and nothing changes. Or you work with us, and we accomplish something that matters."

Elena's expression was unreadable.

"One condition," she said finally.

"Name it."

"I get the exclusive. Whatever happens, whatever you do, I'm the one who tells the story."

Justin smiled.

"Deal."

The story published three weeks later.

Elena Vasquez's exposé on the Voss network ran to forty thousand words. It documented financial connections that spanned continents. It named names that had never been named. It provided the kind of evidence that made denial impossible.

The day it published, Justin and Erik hit the operational infrastructure.

Three facilities raided. Seventeen arrests. Four billion dollars in assets frozen.

The combination was devastating.

Voss's network—the empire he had spent decades building—collapsed in a matter of days.

Elena won a Pulitzer for her reporting.

In her acceptance speech, she thanked the "anonymous sources" who had made the story possible. She didn't mention their names. She never would.

But later, in a bar in Brooklyn, she raised a glass to the two men who had appeared from nowhere and changed everything.

"To the line," she said.

Justin and Erik raised their glasses.

"To the line."

They drank.

And somewhere, in an office that was rapidly becoming a crime scene, Dr. Alaric Voss watched the news coverage and understood that he had underestimated his enemies.

Again.

ETHICS COMMITTEE—VASQUEZ COORDINATION—ASSESSMENT

The Committee notes that coordination with civilian journalists raises significant operational security concerns.

However, the Committee also notes that the Vasquez coordination resulted in the most successful takedown of a criminal network in our operational history.

Assessment: Sometimes unconventional methods produce exceptional results.

Recommendation: Document the approach for potential future use. Note that such coordination requires careful vetting of media partners and should only be attempted when operational objectives align with journalistic interests.

Note from Gerald Morrison: I selected Elena Vasquez. I provided the initial documents. I monitored her progress and alerted Justin and Erik when she was ready.

This was my most significant contribution to their work.

I'm not sure whether to be proud or terrified.

Probably both.

That seems to be a theme.

INTERLUDE

Memo #2,847

Gerald Morrison arrived at the office at 6:15 AM, when the building was empty and the quiet was his.

He made his coffee—black, two sugars, the way his father had made it—and began to write.

INTERNAL MEMORANDUM #2,847
FROM: Gerald Morrison, Senior Analyst
TO: Ethics Review Committee
RE: On the Subject of Patterns
DATE: ■■■■■■■■■■■■■

This memo will not be read.

I have written 2,846 memos before this one. Approximately seven have been read, most by accident. I continue to write them anyway, because the record matters. Someday, someone might want to understand how we got from there to here.

At least one person saw the patterns.

Today I want to write about Lampert and Block.

Not their methods. Everyone writes about their methods. But no one writes about what I see.

What I see is two men who have been doing this for years and have not become monsters.

I have been in oversight for twenty-three years. I have watched people break. Good people who started with principles and ended with something else. The work does that.

Lampert and Block have not drowned.

I don't know how. I don't know why. But I know it matters.

The Mirror Duo didn't understand this.

They thought the violence was the point. They didn't understand that the results come from the stopping—from knowing exactly where the line is and standing on it without crossing over.

David Chen is dead because they didn't understand.

I have written forty-seven memos about verification protocols. No one read them. David Chen is dead, and no one read them.

Gerald finished the memo. Filed it. Knew no one would read it.

He wrote it anyway.

That was the job.

Three weeks later, Justin Lampert sat in Gerald's office.

"You write the memos," Lampert said.

"Yes."

"I read one. Memo 2,847. Someone left it on my desk." He smiled slightly. "The part about the line. About knowing where to stop."

Gerald didn't know what to say.

"Most people think we don't think about it," Lampert continued. "It's not natural. Every single time, there's a moment where you have to choose. And the only thing that makes the choice bearable is knowing that someone, somewhere, is paying attention."

He stood.

"Keep writing the memos, Gerald."

"Why? If no one reads them?"

Lampert turned back.

"Because you notice. When everyone else is looking at results, you're looking at reasons. That's rare. That's worth something."

Then he was gone.

Gerald sat alone, Theodore purring on the desk, and felt something he hadn't felt in years.

Seen.

He started a new memo.

CHAPTER 25

The Analyst's Gambit

Rachel Torres did something she'd been told never to do.

She went alone.

The warehouse in Newark had been on Gerald's radar for three weeks—unusual financial flows, shell company ownership, the kind of patterns that suggested criminal enterprise but never quite confirmed it. Justin and Erik were in Prague, running down the Voss connection. Gerald was buried in data analysis.

But the window was closing. The warehouse was scheduled to be cleaned out in forty-eight hours—records destroyed, personnel relocated, evidence disappeared.

Rachel had two choices: wait for backup and lose the lead, or act and risk everything.

She thought about Harrison Webb. About the thirty-seven people who died because someone decided to wait for the proper channels.

She chose to act.

The security was lighter than expected. Two guards at the entrance, one patrolling the perimeter, a fourth inside monitoring cameras. Professional but not paranoid—these people were confident in their anonymity.

That confidence was their weakness.

Rachel had learned a lot in six months with Justin and Erik. How to move without being seen. How to read a building's vulnerabilities. How to become invisible in plain sight.

But she'd also learned something they hadn't taught her: how to use what she already knew. Analysis wasn't just about patterns on a screen. It was about understanding people—what they expected, what they feared, what they'd never see coming.

She approached the front entrance in a delivery uniform, carrying a clipboard and wearing the bored expression of someone who'd made this stop a hundred times before.

"Package for Hendricks," she said.

The guard frowned. "There's no Hendricks here."

"Look, I just deliver where they tell me. You want to sign, or you want me to mark it undeliverable?"

"We're not expecting any—"

"Fine. Undeliverable." Rachel made a show of checking a box on her clipboard. "Your boss can deal with it."

She turned to leave.

"Wait."

The guard's voice had changed. Curious now instead of dismissive.

"What's in the package?"

"How should I know? I'm just the driver."

She could feel him calculating. A package for someone who didn't exist, at a facility that wasn't supposed to receive packages. It could be a mistake. It could be something else.

Rachel counted the seconds. If he was smart, he'd send her away and report the incident. If he was curious—

"Let me see it."

Curious. Good.

She handed him the package. Inside: a small device, motion-activated, currently displaying a rapid countdown that meant absolutely nothing.

"What the hell is—"

"You have about thirty seconds to evacuate this building," Rachel said, her voice suddenly calm and professional. "That's a chemical dispersal unit. When it reaches zero, everyone inside this facility is going to have a very bad day."

"That's bullshit. You're—"

"Twenty-five seconds."

The guard looked at the countdown. Looked at Rachel. Made a decision.

"EVERYBODY OUT! NOW!"

The evacuation took three minutes and twelve seconds.

Rachel watched from across the street as people poured out of the warehouse—guards, workers, a few men in suits who looked very unhappy about being seen in public. She photographed each of them. Noted license plates. Tracked which direction they fled.

The "chemical dispersal unit" was a kitchen timer attached to a smoke machine. When it went off, it produced a lot of dramatic fog and absolutely nothing dangerous.

But by then, Rachel was already inside.

The records room was exactly where the building schematics said it would be.

Physical files—they'd learned that lesson after Cyprus. Digital records could be hacked, traced, subpoenaed. Paper was still the safest way to keep secrets.

Rachel had fifteen minutes before someone realized the "chemical attack" was a fake. Fifteen minutes to find what she needed.

She started photographing.

Financial records. Names. Dates. Transactions that connected the warehouse to a shipping company that connected to a logistics firm that connected to—

Rachel stopped.

Stared at the name on the document in her hands.

Voss Industries.

She was out of the building in eleven minutes.

By the time the first police cars arrived, she was three blocks away, downloading her photographs to a secure server, already composing the message she would send to Justin and Erik.

Found something. It's bigger than we thought. Voss isn't just watching you—he's building something. And I know what it is.

She paused before sending.

Six months ago, she'd been an analyst who got fired for asking questions. Now she was infiltrating warehouses alone, running ops that would have made her former supervisors faint, and uncovering connections that could take down an empire.

Justin had asked her once why she wanted this. Why she'd given up safety and stability for a life where every day could be her last.

She hadn't known how to answer then.

She did now.

Because this was who she'd always been. Not the analyst who wrote reports that no one read. Not the employee who got fired for doing the right thing. This. The person who saw a warehouse that needed to be hit and hit it. Who trusted her training, her instincts, her ability to adapt.

The person who held the line, even when she was holding it alone.

She sent the message.

Then she disappeared into the Newark night, already planning her next move.

Intercepted communication—Eyes Only

RE: Newark Incident

The warehouse was compromised. Unknown operative, likely connected to Lampert/Block network. They have the financial records linking our shipping operation to the primary infrastructure.

Recommendation: Accelerate timeline. If they're moving this fast, we need to move faster.

Also: Begin file on "Rachel Torres." She wasn't on our radar before. She is now.

Gerald Morrison read the intercepted communication three times.

Then he smiled.

He forwarded the communication to Justin and Erik with a single note:

Rachel went solo. She's good. Maybe better than you were at her stage. But she's on Voss's radar now. Keep her safe.

And tell her I said well done.

CHAPTER 26

The Architect

Dr. Alaric Voss kept a journal.

Not a diary—diaries were for people who wanted to remember their feelings. Voss kept a journal because he believed in documentation. In understanding. In the systematic analysis of everything, including himself.

The journal was handwritten. Digital records could be compromised, hacked, subpoenaed. Paper, in the right conditions, was eternal.

He wrote in it every night, by lamplight, in an office that overlooked a city full of people who would never know his name.

Entry 1,248

Subject: The Morocco Test—Results

The test was successful, in the narrow sense that it provided data. Lampert and Block responded to the water crisis within fourteen hours. They identified the artificial nature of the situation within three hours of arrival. They located and neutralized the saboteur before I expected them to.

But the data raised more questions than it answered. They responded with something that looked like intuition—not pattern recognition, but something else. Something I cannot name.

The phone on his desk buzzed. A message from one of his operatives.

Phase Two ready for implementation. Awaiting authorization.

Voss read the message three times.

Phase Two was the rail system. A slow-motion crisis designed to test whether Lampert and Block would intervene in situations where the threat was systemic rather than immediate. Where there was no single target, no clear villain, no obvious line to hold.

He had designed it carefully. Months of planning. Millions of dollars in bribes and manipulations. All to answer a single question: where did they draw the line between "their problem" and "someone else's problem"?

He typed his response: *Authorized. Proceed.*

Then he returned to his journal.

Entry 1,249

Subject: Hypothesis—The Marcus Hale Variable

I have identified a potential vulnerability.

Marcus Hale. Friend of Lampert. Former colleague. One of the few people in the world who has maintained a genuine personal relationship with either subject.

The standard analysis would suggest that Hale represents leverage. A pressure point. Something that could be used to influence Lampert's behavior.

But I am not interested in leverage.

I am interested in understanding.

What happens when the line is crossed against them? When someone they care about is taken? When the principles they live by are used as weapons?

Do they adapt? Do they break? Do they become something other than what they have been?

These questions require answers.

And answers require... experimentation.

Voss closed the journal.

He sat in silence for a long time, thinking about what he was planning. What it would cost. What it would reveal.

Marcus Hale was a good man. An innocent man, in the sense that mattered. He had done nothing to deserve what was coming.

But Voss had stopped believing in innocence years ago. The world was a system. People were variables. And sometimes, understanding required sacrifice.

He picked up his phone and made a call.

"The Kiev operation," he said. "Move it up. I want it done within the week."

A pause on the other end.

"That's faster than we planned. The preparation—"

"Will be sufficient. The timeline has changed."

He hung up before the operative could object.

Entry 1,250

Subject: Anticipation

In three days, Marcus Hale will be dead.

I do not know this with certainty, of course. Nothing in human behavior is certain. But I have arranged the circumstances. I have created the conditions. I have made his death… probable.

What I do not know is what happens next.

Lampert will grieve. That much is predictable. He is not a machine, whatever his reputation suggests. He has human emotions, human connections, human weaknesses.

But will he change?

Will the loss of someone he cares about alter his principles? Will it move the line, shift the boundary, transform him into something different?

This is what I need to know.

This is why Marcus Hale must die.

Not for any practical purpose. Not to remove a threat or gain an advantage. Simply to observe. To understand. To answer the question that has been haunting me for three years.

Who are they, really?

And what happens when you push them too far?

The operation in Kiev went exactly as planned.

Voss flew to Kiev himself.

This was unusual. He preferred distance—the clean separation of observation from action, the comfort of screens and reports and data that didn't bleed. But this time, distance wasn't enough.

He needed to see.

The safehouse was a Soviet-era apartment on the outskirts of the city. Gray concrete. Barred windows. The kind of building that had witnessed a thousand secrets and would witness a thousand more.

Marcus Hale was inside, bound to a chair, already softened by three hours with Voss's people. His face was swollen. One eye wouldn't open. But he was conscious—Voss had been specific about that.

"Leave us," Voss said.

His operatives exchanged glances but complied. They knew better than to question.

The door closed.

Voss pulled up a chair and sat across from Hale, close enough to see the blood vessels in his remaining good eye.

"You know why you're here."

Hale spat—or tried to. His mouth was too dry. "I don't know anything about Justin's operations."

"I believe you." Voss leaned back, crossing his legs. "That's not why you're here."

"Then what—"

"You're here because you're his friend. His only real friend, as far as I can determine." Voss's voice was clinical, detached. "And I want to know what happens when he loses you."

Understanding dawned in Hale's eye. Not fear for himself—something worse.

"You're using me as an experiment."

"Yes."

"That's—" Hale laughed, and the laugh turned into a cough. "That's genuinely insane."

"Perhaps." Voss stood and walked to the window. "In a few hours, my people will move you to a warehouse. They'll make it look like an ambush—bad intelligence, wrong place, wrong time. Lampert will find you, but not in time. The message we send will draw him out. His response will tell me everything I need to know."

"Justin will come for you."

"Yes. I'm counting on it." Voss turned back. "I want to see what he does with the grief. Whether it changes him. Whether it breaks something that can't be broken by conventional means."

Hale stared at him.

"I've met monsters," Hale said quietly. "I've spent thirty years in intelligence. I've seen what people do to each other in the dark."

"And?"

"You're worse. The others—they do it for money, or power, or because something broke inside them. You're doing this for curiosity." His voice cracked. "You're killing me because you want to take notes."

Voss considered this.

"Yes," he said. "I suppose I am."

He walked to the door and paused.

"For what it's worth, you're not dying for nothing. You're contributing to knowledge. Most people can't say that."

"Go to hell."

Voss smiled—a small, clinical expression that didn't reach his eyes.

"I'll include your final words in my notes."

He left. His operatives would handle the rest.

The experiment had begun.

The intelligence was falsified. The ambush was set. Marcus Hale was in the wrong place at the wrong time because Voss had made sure there was no right place for him to be.

And then Voss watched.

He watched through surveillance feeds and intercepted communications. He watched through operatives positioned to observe without being detected. He watched through every available means, because this was the moment that mattered.

This was the answer he had been seeking.

Entry 1,251

Subject: Observation—Aftermath

Lampert did not break.

I expected rage. I anticipated recklessness. I had prepared for the possibility that he would abandon his principles and come after me with nothing but fury and vengeance.

He did not.

Instead, he mourned. Quietly. Privately. In ways that my observation could not fully capture.

And then he went back to work.

The same methodology. The same principles. The same careful, systematic approach that has defined his entire career.

I do not understand.

I killed his friend. I took something that mattered to him. I crossed the line in the most personal way possible.

And he did not change.

He simply... absorbed it. Integrated it. Made the loss part of himself without letting it alter what he was.

This is either remarkable discipline or genuine conviction. Either he is suppressing his emotions so completely that they do not affect his behavior, or he has found something that allows him to process loss without being destroyed by it.

I do not know which possibility is more disturbing.

Voss closed the journal and sat in darkness.

He had spent three years trying to understand Lampert and Block. Three years of observation and testing and careful experimentation.

And now, finally, he understood.

Not what made them tick. Not how to predict their behavior. Not any of the things he had set out to learn.

He understood that they were real.

He had built his career on the belief that everyone could be modeled. That behavior was the product of incentives and conditioning and predictable responses to predictable stimuli.

But Lampert and Block were not products. They were not responses. They were choices—genuine, authentic choices, made by people who had decided what they believed and committed to living by it.

The line was not a rule they followed.

It was who they were.

And that, Voss realized, made them far more dangerous than he had ever imagined.

Entry 1,252

Subject: Decision

I have made an error.

For three years, I have been studying them as subjects. Observing them. Testing them. Treating them as problems to be solved.

But they are not problems.

They are adversaries.

And I have been so focused on understanding them that I forgot to protect myself from them.

They know I exist now. The Marcus Hale operation revealed too much. They have connected the dots, traced the patterns, identified me as the architect of their suffering.

They are coming.

I could run. I could disappear. I could use the resources I have accumulated to vanish into one of a dozen countries that do not ask questions.

But that would mean admitting defeat.

That would mean accepting that I cannot control them, cannot predict them, cannot reduce them to variables in an equation.

I am not prepared to accept that.

So instead, I will prepare for their arrival.

I will make my office a fortress. I will surround myself with security. I will create conditions that favor my survival.

And when they come—because they will come—I will learn the final lesson.

Whether they can be stopped.

Or whether the line they hold is truly unbreakable.

Voss closed the journal for the last time.

He looked out at the city, at the millions of lives he had spent his career learning to manipulate.

And for the first time in three years, he felt something that his models had not predicted.

Fear.

They were coming.

And he was no longer certain he would survive the encounter.

CHAPTER 27

The Ghosts

The intelligence community told stories about Lampert and Block.

Not official reports—those were classified, sanitized, stripped of anything that might suggest the impossible. But stories. The kind that circulated in bars where operatives drank, in the quiet moments between missions when people allowed themselves to wonder about things that couldn't be officially acknowledged.

The stories sounded like myths.

They were all true.

"Do you ever read what they say about us?" Justin asked once.

They were in a hotel room—another hotel room, one of thousands—reviewing files for an operation that was three days away.

Erik didn't look up from the documents. "No."

"Never?"

"The work is what matters. Not the stories about the work."

Justin considered this. "The stories help, though. They make people hesitate. Make them wonder if the rumors are true."

"Are they?"

"Which rumors?"

Erik did look up then. His expression was unreadable, but something flickered in his eyes that might have been amusement.

"The one about Tokyo. Where we supposedly stopped an assassination by predicting exactly where the shooter would position himself three days in advance."

"That one's exaggerated."

"It was two days."

Justin laughed.

"The one about Mumbai is true," Erik continued. "The hotel. The terrorist attack."

"That wasn't planned. We just happened to be there."

178

"We happened to be there. And because we were there, a hundred and eighty-three people went home to their families."

"We couldn't save everyone."

"No one can save everyone." Erik returned to his documents. "But we saved who we could. That's all anyone can do."

Justin was quiet for a while.

"Do you ever think about what happens when we stop?" he asked finally.

"No."

"Never?"

"Thinking about stopping is how people get killed. You start looking for exits instead of staying focused on the work. You start calculating how much longer, how many more, when you can finally rest."

"That sounds exhausting."

"That's why I don't think about it."

Justin smiled. "You're a very strange person, Erik Block."

"So I've been told."

They returned to their planning.

Outside the window, a city continued its business—people living lives that would never intersect with the shadows where Justin and Erik operated.

That was the point.

That had always been the point.

The line was held so that people never had to know it existed.

CHAPTER 28

The Tests

The rail system in Eastern Europe was Voss's second test.

Not a direct attack—nothing that could be traced to him. Just a series of budget cuts, a cascade of deferred maintenance, a slow accumulation of failures that would eventually result in catastrophe.

He wanted to see if Lampert and Block would intervene.

He wanted to see where they drew their line.

Justin read the intelligence report in a café in Prague.

The data was clear: a rail network deteriorating. Safety systems failing. An accident waiting to happen. The kind of slow-motion disaster that killed people through neglect rather than malice.

"We could do something," Erik said. "Pressure the right people. Expose the corruption."

Justin was quiet for a long time.

"No," he said finally.

Erik looked at him.

"People will get hurt."

"Yes. They will." Justin's voice was steady. "And it's not our responsibility to save them."

"That's not who we are."

"It's exactly who we are." Justin met his partner's eyes. "We can't fix everything. We can't save everyone. If we try, we burn out. We make mistakes. We become the thing we're fighting against."

He gestured at the report.

"This is a systemic problem. Government corruption. Corporate negligence. Decades of bad decisions made by people who knew better. We could fix the immediate crisis—patch the rail system, prevent the accident. But then what? It happens again in six months. A year. The underlying cause remains."

"So we do nothing?"

"No. We do something different."

Justin pulled out his phone.

"We make sure the people who can fix this—the journalists, the regulators, the activists—have what they need to do their jobs. We provide evidence. We apply pressure. We create the conditions for change."

"And if it's not enough?"

Justin was quiet.

"Then we accept that some problems aren't ours to solve," he said. "That our job isn't to fix the world—it's to hold the line. To be there when the system fails completely. To respond to the violations that no one else will address."

Erik considered this.

"We're not gods, Erik," Justin continued. "We're just two men with a particular set of skills and a willingness to use them. If we try to be more than that, we'll destroy ourselves."

Erik nodded slowly.

"Okay," he said. "What's next?"

Voss watched them walk away from the rail crisis.

He watched them provide information to journalists instead of intervening directly. Watched them apply pressure through channels instead of through force.

He made notes.

They had limits.

They could be manipulated.

The third test was more personal.

Voss arranged for the death of Marcus Hale.

Not directly—Voss never acted directly. He provided intelligence to people who wanted Hale dead. He removed the protection that would have kept Hale safe. He created the conditions for an assassination and let human nature do the rest.

Marcus Hale was Justin's friend.

Voss wanted to see what happened when the line was crossed against them.

Justin learned about Marcus's death on a Thursday.

The call came while he was eating breakfast. A simple notification. A name. A date. A cause of death that was listed as "accident" but clearly wasn't.

He set down his phone.

He didn't move for a long time.

Erik found him an hour later, still sitting at the table, still staring at nothing.

"I heard," Erik said.

Justin didn't respond.

"It was an ambush. Intelligence that was either wrong or deliberately falsified. Two minutes that could have gone differently but didn't."

"We should have been there."

"We were following a lead that turned out to be nothing." Erik's voice was quiet. "A distraction. Someone wanted us looking the wrong way."

"Voss?"

"Maybe. Probably."

Justin's hands clenched.

"He's testing us," Justin said. "Has been for months. The water plant. The rail system. Now this."

"What do you want to do?"

Justin didn't answer immediately.

He thought about Marcus. About the years they'd worked together. About the missions, the close calls, the moments of dark humor that made the work bearable.

He thought about what Marcus would want him to do.

"We don't give him what he wants," Justin said finally. "He wants us emotional. Off-balance. Making decisions with our hearts instead of our heads."

"And?"

"We get back to work. We find whoever set this in motion. And we make sure they understand the cost of what they did."

He looked at Erik.

"But we do it our way. On our terms. Without letting him push us into becoming something we're not."

Erik nodded.

"Where do we start?"

Justin smiled. It was not a pleasant smile.

"With Voss," he said. "It's time we had a proper conversation."

Voss received word that they were coming.

He had expected this. Had prepared for it. Had spent three years building toward this moment.

They would come to confront him. To threaten him. To try to stop whatever he was planning.

And he would be ready.

Because this was the final test.

Not of them.

Of everything he had learned.

Erik understood, in the way he understood most things, that the confrontation with Voss would be different.

But there was something else on his mind.

"The journalist," he said.

Justin looked up from the files. "Elena Vasquez?"

"We used her. Fed her information. Put her in danger without her knowledge."

"She's safe now. Her story ran. It made a difference."

"That's not the point."

Justin set down the files. "What is the point?"

"We made the choice for her. Decided she could handle the risk, decided her story was worth the exposure. We treated her like a tool."

"We treated her like an ally."

"Without her consent."

They stared at each other. The silence stretched.

"Sometimes," Justin said carefully, "we have to make decisions for people who don't have all the information."

"That's what the people we hunt say. That's how they justify it."

Justin's jaw tightened. "That's not fair."

"It's not supposed to be fair. It's supposed to be true."

Neither of them spoke.

Erik turned back to the window. Justin returned to the files.

The disagreement hung in the air between them—unresolved, uncomfortable, real.

Some arguments didn't have clean endings.

Some truths didn't fit together neatly.

They would go to confront Voss anyway, because the work required it. But something had shifted between them. A crack in the foundation they'd built over seventeen years.

Small.

But present.

Voss would learn what they were made of soon enough.

One way or another.

CHAPTER 29

The Friend

Marcus Hale was a man who remembered birthdays.

Not in a performative way—not the kind of remembering that came from calendar alerts and assistants. Marcus actually remembered. He would call on your birthday, not text, and he would reference something specific from the previous year. "Did you ever finish that book you were reading?" "How's your sister doing after the surgery?" "Did you figure out the thing with the landlord?"

He remembered because he cared. And in a world full of people who pretended to care, genuine caring was rare enough to be remarkable.

Justin had known Marcus for twelve years. They had served together, briefly, before their careers diverged—Justin into the shadows, Marcus into legitimate intelligence work. Analyst. Good one. The kind of analyst who saw patterns that others missed and asked questions that others wouldn't.

They had dinner twice a year. Always the same restaurant in Georgetown. Always the same booth in the back. Always the same conversation: Marcus pretending not to know what Justin actually did, Justin pretending that the pretending was convincing.

"You look tired," Marcus said, the last time they met.

"I'm always tired."

"More tired than usual." Marcus studied him over the rim of his beer glass. "Whatever you're working on—is it worth it?"

"I think so."

"You think so. Not 'yes.' Not 'definitely.' You think so."

Justin smiled. "You're doing that analyst thing."

"I'm doing that friend thing. There's a difference." Marcus set down his glass. "I worry about you, Justin. Not because of what you do—I've made my peace with not knowing the details. But because of how you look when you do it."

"How do I look?"

185

"Like someone who's forgotten what the other side looks like. Like someone who's been in the dark so long they've stopped believing in light."

The words landed harder than Marcus probably intended. Justin felt them settle in his chest like stones.

"There's still light," he said.

"Yeah?" Marcus's eyes were kind. "When's the last time you saw it?"

Justin didn't have an answer.

That was two months before Marcus died.

The operation was routine.

Marcus was in Kiev, running analysis on a regional trafficking network. Standard work, the kind of thing he'd done a hundred times. Safe, careful, by the book.

He wasn't supposed to be a target.

He wasn't even supposed to be visible.

But someone had made him visible. Someone had put his name on a list. And that list had ended up in the hands of people who used lists to make other lists—shorter lists, final lists, the kind of lists that turned names into past tense.

Justin got the call at 3 AM.

"It's Marcus," the voice said. "You need to come now."

He found Marcus in a warehouse on the outskirts of Kiev.

Erik had tracked the location through channels that didn't bear examination. The drive had taken forty-seven minutes. Every one of them had felt like a year.

The warehouse was quiet when they arrived. Too quiet. The kind of quiet that came after violence, not before it.

Justin went in first.

He found Marcus in a chair in the center of the room.

Still alive.

Barely.

"Hey," Marcus said. His voice was a whisper. A rasp. The sound of someone speaking through damage that speech shouldn't be possible through. "You came."

"Of course I came."

"You shouldn't have. It's a trap."

"I know." Justin knelt beside the chair. Started working on the restraints. "Erik's handling it."

"Erik." Marcus managed something that might have been a laugh. "The quiet one. I always wondered about him."

"Don't talk. Save your strength."

"For what?" Marcus looked at him. His eyes were clear—impossibly clear for someone who had been through what he'd obviously been through. "I'm dying, Justin. We both know it."

"You're not—"

"I'm an analyst, remember? I know what data looks like." Marcus coughed. Blood. Too much blood. "I also know what a message looks like. And this—" He gestured weakly at the room, at himself, at everything. "—this is a message."

"From who?"

"Someone who wanted your attention. Someone who knew that hitting me would hurt you." Marcus's eyes found Justin's. "Someone who's been watching you for a long time."

The restraints came loose.

Justin caught Marcus as he slumped forward. Held him. Felt the labored breathing, the failing heartbeat, the weight of a life that was ending in his arms.

"I need to get you to a hospital."

"Too late for that." Marcus's hand found Justin's arm. Gripped with surprising strength. "Listen. They asked me questions. About you. About Erik. About how you work, what you care about, where your lines are."

"What did you tell them?"

"Nothing. Not because I'm brave—I'm not brave, Justin. I'm just an analyst who got caught up in something beyond my clearance." Marcus coughed again. "I didn't tell them anything because I don't know anything. I never asked. I never wanted to know."

"That probably saved your life."

"That probably extended my death." Marcus smiled. It was awful. "But it doesn't matter. What matters is that someone out there is building a map. Of you. Of what you care about. Of what can be used against you."

"We'll find them."

"I know you will." Marcus's grip weakened. "That's why I'm not scared. Because I know you. And I know that whoever did this—whoever thought they could use me to hurt you—they made a mistake."

"What mistake?"

"They thought hurting your friends would weaken you." Marcus's eyes were drifting closed. "They don't understand. Hurting your friends doesn't make you weak. It makes you certain. It makes you clear. It makes you the thing they should have been afraid of all along."

"Marcus—"

"Find them, Justin." The words were barely audible now. "Find them and show them what happens when they cross the line."

Marcus Hale died at 4:17 AM, in a warehouse in Kiev, in the arms of a friend who had come too late.

Justin held him for a long time after.

He didn't cry. He had trained himself not to cry, years ago, because crying was a luxury that people in his profession couldn't afford.

But he felt it. The loss. The rage. The cold, clear certainty that Marcus had described.

Someone had done this.

Someone had used his friend—his actual friend, one of the few people in the world who knew him as something other than a weapon—as a message.

And messages required responses.

Erik found him twenty minutes later.

"The perimeter is clear. Whoever was here is gone."

"I know."

"We should move. This location is compromised."

"I know."

Erik looked at Marcus's body. At Justin, still holding it.

"I'm sorry," he said.

188

The words were simple. Inadequate. And somehow exactly right.

"He was a good man," Justin said. "He remembered birthdays. He asked about people's lives. He cared about things that didn't matter, because caring was what he did."

"That's why they chose him."

"Yes." Justin stood. Carefully, gently, he laid Marcus's body down. "That's exactly why they chose him."

"What do you want to do?"

Justin looked at his partner.

"I want to find whoever did this. I want to understand why. And then I want to show them what it costs to cross the line against us."

Erik nodded.

"Where do we start?"

Justin thought about the questions Marcus said they'd asked. About the map someone was building. About the patience and planning that this attack suggested.

"We start with the patterns," he said. "Someone has been watching us. Studying us. This wasn't random—it was calculated. Precise. The work of someone who thinks they understand how we operate."

"And they think killing your friend will throw us off."

"They think it will make us emotional. Careless. Predictable."

"Will it?"

Justin looked at Marcus one last time.

"No," he said. "It will make us thorough."

They left the warehouse as the sun was coming up.

Behind them, Marcus Hale's body waited for the authorities who would eventually find it, document it, and file it under "unsolved."

Ahead of them, a hunt was beginning.

The kind of hunt that would end with someone understanding exactly what it meant to cross the line.

We are the consequences.

The words had never felt more true.

PART FOUR

The Line Holds

"Every line eventually gets tested. The ones that matter are the ones that hold."

— Gerald Morrison, Memo #2,891

"We are the consequences."

— The Line

CHAPTER 30

The Chess Game

Dr. Alaric Voss played chess every Thursday evening.

Not because he enjoyed the game—though he did, in the abstract way he enjoyed all systems of rules and consequences. He played because it gave him time to think. The ritual of moving pieces across a board, considering positions seven moves ahead, allowed his mind to work on other problems.

Tonight, the other problem was Lampert and Block.

His opponent was a professor of mathematics at Georgetown. A brilliant man. Completely unaware that he was sitting across from someone who had orchestrated the deaths of three people in the past month alone.

"Your move," the professor said.

Voss looked at the board.

The position was complex. His knight was threatened. His bishop was pinned. The professor was three moves away from a devastating attack on his king.

And yet.

Voss moved his pawn.

One square forward. An insignificant move. A move that the professor would dismiss as defensive, reactive, desperate.

The professor smiled and captured Voss's knight.

"Interesting choice," the professor said.

"Sometimes the interesting choices are the ones that don't make sense immediately."

The game continued.

Voss sacrificed his bishop. Then a rook. Then another pawn.

The professor's smile faded. He began to see what Voss was building—a position that looked weak but was actually inevitable. A trap that had been set fifteen moves earlier and was only now becoming visible.

"Checkmate in four," Voss said quietly.

The professor studied the board.

His face went pale.

"I don't… how did you…"

"You were focused on the pieces I was losing," Voss explained. "You weren't paying attention to the position I was creating."

He reset the board.

"Same time next week?"

Voss drove home through streets that were empty in the way that Washington streets were empty at night—not truly empty, just populated by different people. The ones who worked while others slept. The ones who made decisions that would never be recorded.

His mind was still on the chess game.

Not the one he had played. The one he was playing with Lampert and Block.

They were pieces on his board, whether they knew it or not. Every operation they ran, every target they neutralized, every line they held—it was all data. Information that Voss could use to build models, predict behavior, identify vulnerabilities.

The Morocco test had taught him about their response time. The rail system had taught him about their priorities. The Marcus Hale operation had taught him about their capacity for grief.

Now it was time for the next lesson.

MEMO (PRIVATE)

SUBJECT: Project Calibration—Phase Four

Date: [REDACTED]

The previous phases have provided valuable data. I now understand their methodology, their principles, their psychological patterns.

What I do not understand is their network.

Lampert and Block do not operate alone. They have resources—intelligence, logistics, funding—that exceed what any two individuals could reasonably possess. Someone is helping them. Someone with access to information that should be impossible to obtain.

Phase Four will identify this network.

The approach is simple: I will create a situation that requires them to reach out to their contacts. I will observe who responds. I will map the connections.

And then I will have leverage.

Not against them directly—direct confrontation with Lampert and Block is inadvisable. But against the people who support them. The infrastructure that makes their work possible.

Remove the infrastructure, and they become isolated.

Isolated, they become vulnerable.

Vulnerable, they can be controlled.

The situation Voss created was elegant in its simplicity.

A journalist in Berlin had been investigating corporate corruption. She had accumulated evidence that would destroy several major companies—companies that were connected to networks Voss had built relationships with over the years.

The journalist was a threat to many people.

Voss made sure that Lampert and Block would learn of her existence.

He made sure they would learn that she was in danger.

And then he watched.

Gerald Morrison's phone rang at 2 AM.

He fumbled for it in the darkness, dislodging Theodore from his position on the pillow.

"Yes?"

"Gerald. It's Justin."

Gerald sat up immediately. In twenty-three years of government service, he had received exactly four calls from field operatives. All four had been emergencies.

"What's happening?"

"I need information. A journalist in Berlin. Katarina Müller. She's been investigating Hartwell Pharmaceuticals and several connected companies."

"I know the name. She's been making enemies."

"Someone's planning to silence her. We need to get to her first."

Gerald was already moving to his laptop.

"I can have a preliminary workup in three hours. Full background, known associates, current location."

"Make it two."

"Justin—"

"Two hours, Gerald. She doesn't have three."

The line went dead.

Gerald started working.

Three thousand miles away, Voss smiled.

He had positioned a surveillance team near Gerald Morrison's apartment months ago. Not because he suspected Morrison specifically—he had teams positioned near dozens of potential contacts. Insurance against exactly this situation.

Now one of those teams was reporting activity.

Lights turning on at 2 AM. Shadows moving behind curtains. The particular energy of someone who had just received urgent news.

Morrison.

The analyst who wrote memos no one read.

Voss hadn't considered him seriously before. Morrison was a bureaucrat. A paper-pusher. The kind of person who observed without acting.

But apparently, Morrison had found a way to act.

The next call came four hours later.

Gerald's voice was tired but precise.

"Katarina Müller. Forty-three years old. Investigative journalist for Der Spiegel. Currently working on an exposé about pharmaceutical companies suppressing safety data."

"Where is she now?"

"Berlin. An apartment in Kreuzberg. But she's not alone."

Justin's voice sharpened. "What do you mean?"

"There's surveillance on her building. Professional. The kind of surveillance that suggests someone with resources is paying attention."

"Can you identify who?"

A pause. Gerald's keyboard clicking.

"The surveillance team is using equipment that matches a signature we've seen before. The same equipment was used in Morocco. And in Vienna."

Justin was quiet.

"Voss."

"I can't confirm, but the pattern suggests—"

"It's Voss. He's watching her. Which means he's watching us."

"Justin, if he knows about the connection—"

"He doesn't know about you, Gerald. Not yet. And we're going to keep it that way."

"How?"

"By giving him something else to look at."

The operation in Berlin was a masterpiece of misdirection.

Justin and Erik didn't approach Katarina Müller directly. Instead, they created a series of false leads—fake contacts, fabricated intelligence, the kind of noise that would occupy anyone trying to track their movements.

While the noise was happening, Gerald arranged for Müller to be extracted through channels that had nothing to do with Lampert and Block. A friend of a friend. A journalist who owed Gerald a favor from a story he had helped kill fifteen years ago.

Müller was in London before Voss's surveillance team realized she was gone.

MEMO (PRIVATE)

SUBJECT: Project Calibration—Phase Four Assessment

Date: [REDACTED]

The Berlin operation did not proceed as anticipated.

Müller was extracted, but not through Lampert and Block's usual channels. Someone else was involved. Someone who understood my observation protocols well enough to route around them.

This is concerning.

Lampert and Block are being more careful than expected. Or their network is more sophisticated than I realized.

Either way, the game has changed.

I need to adjust my approach.

Gerald Morrison sat in his office, Theodore on his lap, staring at a screen full of data.

He had helped extract a journalist from danger. He had done something that mattered—something beyond writing memos that no one read.

And he had done it without revealing himself to whoever was watching.

But for how long?

Voss—or whoever was orchestrating this—was smart. Patient. The kind of adversary who would eventually find every thread, follow every connection, identify every ally.

Gerald was in the game now.

There was no going back.

He reached for his phone and typed a message to Justin:

She's safe. But we need to talk. Someone is mapping your network.

The response came thirty seconds later:

We know. And we have a plan.

Gerald looked at Theodore.

"Well," he said. "It seems I've chosen a side."

Theodore purred.

Outside, the sun was rising over Washington. Another day beginning. Another set of choices to be made.

Gerald Morrison had made his.

Now he would have to live with the consequences.

CHAPTER 31

The System Fights Back

The first sign of coordinated resistance came in Berlin.

Justin was meeting a contact—a mid-level bureaucrat in the German intelligence services who had been feeding them information for three years. Standard procedure. Monthly check-in. Nothing unusual.

Except the contact didn't show.

And the café where they were supposed to meet had new management.

And the new management had eyes that tracked Justin's movements with professional interest.

"Burned," Erik said quietly, from his position at a table near the window.

"Looks like it."

"Exit?"

"Back door. Thirty seconds."

They moved.

The back door led to an alley. The alley was not empty.

Three men. Professional. Armed. Waiting.

"Well," Justin said. "This is new."

The fight lasted ninety seconds.

Not because the men were incompetent—they weren't. They had training. Coordination. The kind of backup that suggested significant resources.

But they weren't Erik and Justin.

When it was over, two of the men were unconscious and the third was zip-tied to a drainpipe, answering questions he had been trained not to answer.

"Who sent you?" Justin asked.

The man's jaw was set. Stubborn. The kind of resistance that came from believing in something.

"You're not going to talk," Justin observed. "You've been trained. You've been motivated. You believe you're on the right

197

side."

The man didn't respond.

Justin crouched in front of him.

"Here's what's going to happen," he said. "We're going to walk away. We're going to disappear. And you're going to report back to whoever sent you that the operation failed."

"You can't—"

"I can. I have. I will." Justin's voice was calm. "But here's the part you should pay attention to: I'm not going to hurt you. I'm not going to punish you for doing your job. I'm going to let you go, and you're going to live, because that's how we operate."

He leaned closer.

"Ask yourself if the people who sent you would do the same."

He stood.

"Erik. Let's go."

They disappeared into the Berlin night.

Behind them, the man struggled against his restraints and wondered why he was still alive.

The coordinated resistance wasn't random.

Over the next six weeks, they identified seventeen separate incidents—burned contacts, compromised safe houses, operations that went sideways in ways that suggested inside information.

Someone was feeding their enemies.

Someone was building walls.

"Voss," Erik said.

"Maybe." Justin was studying the pattern—the timing, the locations, the specific details that had been compromised. "But Voss is in prison. His network is dismantled."

"His ideas aren't."

Justin nodded slowly.

That was the problem with people like Voss. You could lock them up. You could tear down everything they'd built. But the ideas persisted. The methodology spread. The belief that the system could be controlled through manipulation—that belief didn't require its creator to function.

"Someone's continuing his work," Justin said.

"Or someone was always working parallel to him."

"Either way, we have a problem."

Erik moved to the window.

"What do you want to do?"

Justin thought about it.

The old approach would be direct confrontation. Find the source. Eliminate the threat. Move on.

But this was different. This was systemic. This was an immune response—the system defending itself against the people trying to change it.

"We adapt," Justin said finally. "We change our patterns. We find new contacts, new channels, new ways to operate."

"That takes time."

"I know."

"And while we're rebuilding, the people we were trying to stop keep doing what they're doing."

"I know that too."

Justin looked at his partner.

"But rushing gets us killed. And dead, we can't help anyone."

Erik considered this.

"The line," he said.

"The line."

"We hold it."

"We hold it." Justin's expression eased. "Even when holding it means stepping back."

The rebuilding took three months.

Three months of careful work. New contacts vetted through multiple channels. New safe houses established in locations that couldn't be traced. New operational protocols that accounted for the leaks, the compromises, the systematic effort to shut them down.

It was frustrating.

It was necessary.

And slowly, piece by piece, they put themselves back together.

The breakthrough came from an unexpected source.

Gerald Morrison sent a message through channels that weren't supposed to exist.

I found something. Meet me.

Justin read the message three times.

Gerald Morrison was an analyst. He wrote memos that no one read. He had never, in twenty-three years, reached out directly to anyone in the field.

Something had changed.

They met in a park in Virginia.

Gerald looked different than Justin remembered—older, more tired, carrying a weight that hadn't been there before.

"You took a risk reaching out," Justin said.

"I know." Gerald's voice was quiet. "But I found something you need to see."

He handed over a tablet. On the screen: documents, communication intercepts, financial records.

"The resistance you've been facing," Gerald said. "The coordinated effort to shut you down. It's not random. It's not multiple actors working independently."

"One source?"

"One committee." Gerald pointed to a section of the documents. "Look at the authorization structure. Look at the funding channels. Look at the timeline."

Justin looked.

He saw what Gerald was showing him.

"This goes to the top," Justin said quietly.

"Higher than you'd believe." Gerald's expression was grim. "The people trying to shut you down—they're not criminals you've exposed. They're not networks you've dismantled. They're the people who are supposed to be on your side."

"The system."

"The system is fighting back. Not because you're wrong—they know you're right. They're fighting back because you're effective. Because you're changing things. Because you're proving that it's possible to hold people accountable."

Gerald took back the tablet.

"They can't stop the idea," he said. "So they're trying to stop the men."

Justin took his time responding.

"Why are you telling us this?"

"Because I write memos that no one reads," Gerald said. "Because I've spent twenty-three years noticing things that other people ignore. Because—"

He stopped.

"Because the record matters," Justin finished.

Gerald nodded.

"Someone has to see. Someone has to document. And someone has to act."

He looked at Justin.

"I've done the seeing and the documenting. The acting is up to you."

They parted ways at the edge of the park.

Justin watched Gerald walk away—back to his office, back to his cat, back to the endless work of noticing things that no one wanted noticed.

"He's brave," Erik said.

"He doesn't think so."

"That's what makes it brave."

Justin considered this.

He thought about the documents Gerald had shown them. About the systematic effort to shut them down. About the realization that their enemies weren't just the criminals they exposed—they were the institutions that were supposed to protect people.

"This changes things," he said.

"Yes."

"We can't fight everyone."

"No."

Justin looked at the sky.

"But we can make them choose," he said. "Force them to decide which side they're on. Make the line so clear that no one can pretend they don't see it."

"How?"

Justin smiled.

"We do what we always do," he said. "We find problems. We solve them. We hold the line."

"That's not an answer."

"No," Justin agreed. "But it's the truth."

They walked away from the park, into a city that was full of people who had decided which side of the line they stood on.

Most of them had chosen wrong.

But some—a few, here and there, scattered through the system like seeds in concrete—had chosen right.

Gerald Morrison was one of them.

And that, Justin thought, was enough to keep going.

One person at a time.

One choice at a time.

One line at a time.

Until the lines connected.

Until the choices added up.

Until somewhere, somehow, the balance shifted.

That was the work.

That was always the work.

And they would keep doing it until they couldn't anymore.

CHAPTER 32

The Decision

Gerald Morrison had kept secrets for twenty-three years.

This was, in some ways, the core function of his job. An analyst's work was secrets—gathering them, cataloging them, understanding them, protecting them. Gerald had built his career on the ability to know things that others didn't, and to keep that knowledge safe.

But he had never kept secrets from his own organization before.

Now he was keeping the biggest secret of his career.

The file on his desk was thin. Deliberately thin. Gerald had learned early that thick files attracted attention, and attention was the last thing this file could afford.

SUBJECT: Personal Reference Materials

CLASSIFICATION: None

Inside: everything Gerald knew about Lampert and Block's network. The contacts. The channels. The invisible infrastructure that made their work possible.

And his own place in it.

He was part of something now. Not just an observer. Not just an analyst who wrote memos that no one read. He was a node in a network that operated outside every official structure.

The realization was terrifying.

It was also exhilarating.

Gerald gathered the papers on his desk. He had been working on a memo—his 2,853rd—about a pattern he had identified in global financial flows. Money moving through channels that suggested coordination. A network that was either working toward something or falling apart.

The memo would be filed. It would not be read. It would join the thousands of other memos that documented things that mattered without actually mattering themselves.

But this time, Gerald had an alternative.

He could share the information with Justin.

The decision seemed simple on the surface.

Share information that could help people who were doing good work. What was wrong with that?

Everything, according to the rules Gerald had spent twenty-three years following.

The information was classified. Sharing it with unauthorized parties was a federal crime. Career-ending at best. Prison at worst.

But the rules had also allowed Henry Lau to traffic children for fifteen years while law enforcement agencies filed paperwork.

The rules had allowed Hartwell Pharmaceuticals to hide data that killed twelve people.

The rules had allowed Voss to orchestrate the deaths of innocent people in pursuit of some agenda that Gerald didn't fully understand.

The rules, Gerald was beginning to realize, were not the same as justice.

He made his decision at 3:47 AM on a Tuesday.

The specific time didn't matter. But Gerald noted it anyway, because he was an analyst and analysts noted things. He would remember this moment—the exact second when he stopped being a passive observer and became an active participant.

He typed a message to Justin:

I have information about a financial network. The patterns suggest coordination at the highest levels. This may be connected to Voss.

The response came four minutes later:

Can you meet?

Same place. Tomorrow. 8 AM.

The park was cold at 8 AM.

Gerald sat on the same bench where they had met before, holding a coffee he had no intention of drinking. The cold was bracing. It kept him alert. It reminded him that this was real—not a thought experiment, not a theoretical exercise, but an actual choice with actual consequences.

Justin arrived alone.

"No Erik?"

"He's watching from a distance." Justin sat beside him. "You said something about a financial network."

Gerald opened his briefcase and removed the thin file.

"I've been tracking money flows for six months," he said. "Nothing official—just patterns I noticed in routine analysis. Money moving through unusual channels. Accounts that shouldn't exist. Transactions that suggest coordination across multiple organizations."

"What kind of coordination?"

"The kind that looks like noise until you see it from high enough." Gerald handed over the file. "There's a network. Bigger than anything I've seen before. It touches everything—government, business, criminal organizations. And at the center of it—"

"Voss."

"Maybe. Probably." Gerald shook his head. "I can't prove it. But the patterns are consistent with someone who's building something. Not just making money. Building infrastructure. Creating a system."

Justin studied the documents.

"This is good," he said. "Better than good. This fills gaps we didn't know we had."

"There's more." Gerald hesitated. "I know you've been careful. I know you've tried to keep me protected. But Voss is mapping your network. He's patient. Eventually, he'll find me."

"We won't let that happen."

"You can't promise that."

Justin looked at him.

"No," he admitted. "I can't. But I can promise that we'll do everything possible to keep you safe. And if something does happen—if you're ever exposed—we'll get you out."

"Out?"

"New identity. New location. The same thing we've done for dozens of people who've helped us over the years."

Gerald considered this.

"I'm sixty-one years old," he said. "I have a cat and a sister who makes me come to Sunday dinner. I've lived in the same apartment for eighteen years."

"Is that a no?"

"It's a context." Gerald smiled tiredly. "I've spent my entire career in the background. Reading reports. Writing memos. Noticing things that other people are too busy to notice. I never expected to matter."

He looked at Justin.

"But I think I matter now. To you. To the work. To whatever it is we're trying to accomplish."

"You do."

"Then I'll keep helping. Whatever the consequences."

Justin nodded slowly.

"Thank you, Gerald."

"Don't thank me yet." Gerald stood. "Thank me when we've actually accomplished something."

He walked away, leaving Justin alone on the bench.

Behind him, twenty-three years of careful anonymity were ending.

Ahead of him, something new was beginning.

Gerald didn't know what it was.

But for the first time in decades, he was looking forward to finding out.

ETHICS COMMITTEE—PERSONNEL CONCERNS

SUBJECT: Morrison, Gerald—Behavioral Assessment

STATUS: Ongoing

The Committee has noted some unusual activity patterns in Analyst Morrison's recent work:

1. Increased access to classified databases outside his normal areas of responsibility

>

2. Extended work hours, particularly during periods when other staff are absent

>

3. Communications with encrypted devices that do not appear in official logs

Assessment: Morrison has been a model employee for twenty-three years. His record is spotless. His contributions to analysis have been valuable, if underappreciated.

However, the recent changes in his behavior warrant observation.

Recommendation: Continue monitoring. Do not confront directly without evidence of actual wrongdoing.

Note: This recommendation assumes that "wrongdoing" has a clear definition. In Morrison's case, we're not certain it does. He may simply be doing the work we should have been doing all along.

We're not sure if that's a problem or a solution.

Gerald returned to his office and found Theodore asleep on his keyboard.

"You're going to delete something important," Gerald said.

Theodore did not respond.

Gerald moved the cat and looked at the screen.

A new message from Justin:

The financial data is exactly what we needed. We're moving on Voss's network within the week.

Stay safe, Gerald. And thank you.

Gerald read the message twice.

Then he deleted it.

Then he started writing a new memo—his 2,854th—about patterns in financial intelligence that suggested large-scale coordination across multiple sectors.

The memo would be filed.

It would not be read.

But this time, that was exactly what Gerald wanted.

The work continued.

The line held.

And somewhere in a small office in a building that most people didn't know existed, an analyst with a cat and too many memos was finally making a difference.

It wasn't heroic.

It wasn't dramatic.

But it was necessary.

And that, Gerald was learning, was the only thing that truly mattered.

CHAPTER 33

The Network

Money leaves trails.

This was the fundamental truth of modern crime that Justin had learned early in his career. You can hide bodies. You can destroy evidence. You can silence witnesses. But money—money moves through systems, leaves records, creates patterns that persist long after the crime itself has been forgotten.

The network they had discovered in the Berlin aftermath was not a single operation.

It was an ecosystem.

Dozens of shell companies. Hundreds of transactions. Thousands of individual decisions that added up to something ugly and profitable.

"This is bigger than Voss," Erik said, studying the data they'd extracted. "Bigger than anything we've seen."

Justin nodded. "They learned from watching us. They decentralized. No single point of failure."

"Which means no single point of attack."

"Which means we need to be creative."

Erik looked at him. "Define 'creative.'"

Justin smiled.

"I thought you'd never ask."

The first target was a banker in Geneva.

His name was Heinrich Müller, and he had spent thirty years pretending to be respectable. He wore conservative suits. He attended the right parties. He donated to the right charities. He was, by all appearances, exactly what a Swiss banker was supposed to be.

He was also the financial architect of three major criminal networks.

Not the head—networks like this didn't have heads, that was the point. But Müller was the one who designed the structures. The one who created the shell companies, established the channels, made the money move in ways that couldn't be traced.

He was, in his own way, an artist.

Justin could respect that.

He could also destroy it.

They found Müller in his office at 3 AM.

The man kept unusual hours—another eccentricity that his colleagues attributed to genius and his wife attributed to avoiding her. He was behind his desk, reviewing documents that would never see the light of day, when the lights went out.

And came back on.

And Justin was sitting across from him.

"Good evening, Herr Müller."

Müller didn't panic. That was interesting. Most people panicked when strangers appeared in their secure offices at 3 AM. Müller just looked up, assessed the situation, and began calculating options.

"You're not here to kill me," he said. It wasn't a question.

"What makes you say that?"

"If you wanted me dead, I would be dead. You're here to talk."

Justin smiled. "Very good. Most people take longer to figure that out."

"I am not most people."

"No. You're not." Justin leaned forward. "Which is why I'm giving you a choice."

Müller's eyes narrowed. "What kind of choice?"

"The kind that determines whether you spend the rest of your life in a Swiss prison or a beach in a country without extradition."

"I don't understand."

"Yes, you do." Justin pulled out a tablet. "This is your life's work. Every transaction. Every shell company. Every dirty dollar that's passed through your hands in the last thirty years."

Müller's face went pale.

"That's impossible. My systems are—"

"Your systems are very good. We're better." Justin set the tablet on the desk. "Here's the choice: you can help us dismantle the networks you've created, provide evidence against the people who use them, and disappear into comfortable anonymity. Or you can refuse, and this information goes to every law enforcement agency in Europe."

"If I cooperate, I'm a dead man."

"If you don't cooperate, you're a dead man in prison." Justin shrugged. "I'm offering you a chance to be a dead man on a beach. The choice is yours."

Müller stared at him.

"Why?" he asked finally. "Why give me a choice at all? You could destroy me without asking."

"Because that's not what we do." Justin stood. "We're not executioners, Herr Müller. We're not judges. We're just two people who believe that everyone—even people like you—deserves a chance to make a different choice."

He walked to the door.

"You have twenty-four hours. Use them wisely."

Müller cooperated.

Not because he had a change of heart—men like Müller didn't have changes of heart. He cooperated because the math made sense. Because the alternative was worse. Because, in the end, self-interest was more powerful than loyalty.

The information he provided was extraordinary.

Account numbers. Access codes. The names and locations of people who had thought they were untouchable. Three decades of secrets, handed over in a single encrypted file.

"This is everything," Müller said, when he delivered it. "Every network I've built. Every client I've served. My entire life's work."

Justin took the file.

"It's a start," he said.

"A start?"

"This brings down fifty people. Maybe a hundred. But the system that created them is still standing." Justin looked at Müller with something that might have been respect. "You're the architect. You know better than anyone how these structures work. How they regenerate. How they adapt."

Müller nodded slowly.

"They'll rebuild," he said. "Within a year, two years, there will be new networks. New architects. New ways of moving money that can't be traced."

"I know."

"So what's the point?"

Justin thought about the question.

He thought about David Chen, the accountant who had died for noticing something wrong.

He thought about Sarah Okonkwo, the whistleblower who had almost died for speaking up.

He thought about all the people—the anonymous, the invisible, the ordinary—who had tried to do the right thing and been crushed by systems that were bigger than they were.

"The point," Justin said, "is that we keep going anyway. That we hold the line, even when we know it's going to shift. That we do the work, even when we know it's never finished."

He looked at Müller.

"Because the alternative is surrender. And we don't surrender."

Müller disappeared three days later.

New identity. New life. A beach somewhere warm, probably, where he could spend his remaining years wondering whether he'd made the right choice.

The networks he'd built collapsed within weeks.

Fifty-three arrests across seven countries. $2.4 billion in assets seized. The largest coordinated financial crime prosecution in European history.

And somewhere in the chaos, a message was being received.

The line existed.

It was enforceable.

And crossing it had consequences.

ETHICS COMMITTEE—INTERNAL REVIEW

Subject: Operation Müller

Status: Successful (Retroactively Sanctioned)

The Committee notes that Agents Lampert and Block conducted this operation without prior authorization, without official oversight, and without regard for approximately seventeen different international treaties.

The Committee also notes that the operation resulted in the largest financial crime prosecution in European history.

Recommendation: No disciplinary action. Please stop asking us to discipline them. It doesn't work.

Note from Gerald: I wrote twelve memos predicting that decentralized financial crime would become the primary threat vector within five years. No one read them. Lampert and Block figured it out anyway. I'm not sure whether to be proud or irritated.

Second note from Gerald: Both. I'm both.

Erik cleaned his weapon in the silence after the operation.

The ritual was meaningless—modern weapons didn't require the maintenance. But there was something meditative in the process. Disassembly. Inspection. Reassembly of parts that fit together with mechanical precision.

Seventeen years.

The number surfaced unbidden. Seventeen years since he had started this work.

He thought about the targets. Not the ones they'd stopped—those were documented, catalogued, filed away. He thought about the ones they'd missed. The operations that came too late. The patterns they hadn't seen until the damage was done.

There was a girl in São Paulo whose case file still sat in his memory. Twelve years old. Taken before they'd identified the network. Found after—but "after" was a word that covered multitudes. After could mean a day. After could mean a lifetime.

For her, it had been three months.

She was alive now. In a recovery program. Getting help.

But Erik remembered her eyes in the photograph. Before and after. The same face, technically. The same girl.

Not the same person.

That's the cost, he thought. *Not the ones we save. The ones we almost save. The ones where "almost" has to be enough because it's all there is.*

Justin could sleep after operations. Justin had a gift for compartmentalization, for putting the work in a box and living outside it.

Erik couldn't.

But he'd learned to use it. The inability to forget became a kind of fuel. Every face he remembered was a reason to move faster next time. Every "almost" was an argument against hesitation.

Seventeen years.

How many more?

However many it took.

He finished cleaning the weapon, set it aside, and started planning the next operation.

The work continued.

The work always continued.

CHAPTER 34

The Network Revealed

Voss discovered Gerald Morrison on a Tuesday.

Not through surveillance—Morrison was too careful for that. Not through informants—Morrison had spent twenty-three years building relationships that were impenetrable to outside influence.

Through analysis.

The breakthrough came from a pattern Voss had been studying for months.

Lampert and Block's intelligence was too good. Too specific. Too perfectly timed. They knew things they shouldn't know. They anticipated moves they shouldn't be able to anticipate.

Someone was feeding them information.

Voss had assumed the source was external—a contact in a foreign intelligence service, perhaps, or a hacker with access to classified systems. He had spent considerable resources pursuing these possibilities.

All of them had been dead ends.

Which meant the source was internal.

Someone inside the American intelligence community was working with Lampert and Block.

Voss approached the problem systematically.

He compiled a list of everyone who had access to the kind of intelligence Lampert and Block had demonstrated. Seven hundred names. He cross-referenced against everyone who had shown unusual behavior patterns in the past year. That reduced the list to one hundred and twelve.

He analyzed communication patterns, travel records, financial transactions. He looked for anomalies—the small deviations from routine that suggested someone was doing something they shouldn't be doing.

The list narrowed to twenty-three.

He examined each of the twenty-three in detail. Their careers. Their relationships. Their psychological profiles.

One name stood out.

Gerald Morrison.

PROFILE: Morrison, Gerald

Position: Senior Analyst, [REDACTED]

Tenure: 23 years

Performance: Exceptional (documented), Undervalued (inferred)

Notes: Morrison is an institutional fixture. He has survived multiple reorganizations, budget cuts, and leadership changes. His survival is attributed to competence, discretion, and a complete lack of ambition.

Anomalies:

• *Increased database access outside normal patterns (past 8 months)*

>

• *Extended work hours correlating with Lampert/Block operational activity*

>

• *Known cat in secure facility (security violation, consistently ignored)*

>

• *Memos demonstrating awareness of patterns that exceed official analysis*

Assessment: Morrison has the access, the capability, and—most interestingly—the motivation. His memos reveal deep frustration with institutional inaction. He believes the system is failing. He believes someone should be doing more.

Conclusion: Morrison is the source.

Voss considered his options.

He could expose Morrison. Send evidence to the appropriate authorities. Watch as a twenty-three-year career was destroyed and an old man was sent to prison.

But that would be wasteful.

Morrison was valuable. Not as an enemy—as a resource. Someone with his access, his analytical capabilities, his obvious dedication to doing what he believed was right... that was too useful to destroy.

The question was how to use him.

MEMO (PRIVATE)

SUBJECT: Morrison Option—Analysis

Date: [REDACTED]

Exposure is not optimal. It removes Morrison from play but provides no lasting advantage. Lampert and Block will simply find another source.

Alternative approaches:

Option 1: Recruitment

Approach Morrison directly. Offer him something he wants—influence, resources, the ability to make a real difference. Turn him from their asset to mine.

Risk: Morrison's apparent idealism may be genuine. He may refuse. Worse, he may alert Lampert and Block to my awareness.

Probability of success: 23%

Option 2: Manipulation

Use Morrison without his knowledge. Feed information through channels he monitors. Shape his analysis to serve my purposes.

Risk: Morrison is too skilled an analyst to be manipulated indefinitely. Eventually, he will notice the patterns.

Probability of success: 47%

Option 3: Leverage

Gather evidence of Morrison's activities. Hold it in reserve. Use the threat of exposure to control his behavior at a crucial moment.

Risk: Leverage requires timing. Too early, and Morrison becomes useless. Too late, and the opportunity passes.

Probability of success: 71%

Recommendation: Option 3. Gather evidence. Wait for the optimal moment.

Voss began gathering evidence.

It was not difficult. Morrison had been careful, but careful was not invisible. There were traces—encrypted communications that could be correlated with Lampert/Block operations, database queries that suggested awareness of classified activities, the accumulated fingerprints of a man who was doing something he shouldn't be doing.

Voss documented everything.

He organized it into a file that would destroy Morrison's career, his freedom, and everything he had built over twenty-three years.

And then he waited.

The waiting was the hardest part.

Voss was not a patient man by nature. He was a man who saw problems and solved them, who identified inefficiencies and corrected them, who understood that action was almost always preferable to inaction.

But this situation required patience.

Morrison was useful to Lampert and Block. As long as that usefulness continued, Voss could observe, could learn, could map the connections that would eventually allow him to dismantle everything they had built.

The moment to strike would come.

When it did, Voss would be ready.

In his small office, Gerald Morrison was unaware that he had been identified.

He continued his work. Continued his memos. Continued his quiet collaboration with men who were trying to change the world.

"There's a pattern. I can almost see it. Someone is watching us. Watching them. Preparing for something."

He looked at his screen—at the data that had been his life's work, at the patterns that most people were too busy to notice.

"But I don't know what."

Gerald returned to work.

The clock on his wall ticked steadily toward a confrontation he couldn't yet imagine.

And somewhere else, in an office that overlooked a city full of unsuspecting people, Alaric Voss smiled and added another page to a file that would change everything.

The game continued.

The pieces moved.
And the checkmate drew closer with every passing day.

CHAPTER 35

The Line Becomes Enforceable

Diana Cross was a titan of industry.

That was the phrase journalists used, and Diana had always found it amusing. Titans were gods. She was just a woman who had learned early that the world belonged to people who took it.

She had taken quite a lot.

Pharmaceutical companies. Real estate developments. Media conglomerates. A portfolio of power that stretched across continents and touched millions of lives.

Most of those lives were improved by her work. Jobs created. Medicines developed. Housing built.

Some of them were not.

Diana preferred not to think about those.

Her office occupied the top floor of a building she owned in Manhattan. Floor-to-ceiling windows. Art that belonged in museums. The kind of space that announced: I have arrived, and I have no intention of leaving.

She was reviewing quarterly reports when her assistant's voice came through the intercom.

"Ms. Cross? There are two men here to see you. They don't have an appointment."

Diana frowned. She didn't see people without appointments. Appointments were how civilized people operated.

"Tell them to schedule through my office."

A pause.

"Ms. Cross, they say it's about Hartwell."

Diana's blood went cold.

Hartwell Pharmaceuticals. The company that had been destroyed three months ago. The company that had been connected to her through six layers of shell corporations and three different jurisdictions.

The connection that was supposed to be untraceable.

"Send them in."

Justin Lampert and Erik Block entered Diana Cross's office like they owned it.

This irritated Diana more than she wanted to admit. She was used to being the most powerful person in any room. These two men didn't seem to have received that memo.

"Ms. Cross," the talkative one said. "Thank you for seeing us."

"I don't believe I had a choice." Diana remained behind her desk. The desk was important. It was a barrier. A statement. A reminder of who was in charge. "You mentioned Hartwell."

"Hartwell Pharmaceuticals. Destroyed three months ago. CEO arrested. Board dissolved. Assets seized."

"I read about it in the papers. Tragic situation."

"Tragic." The man smiled. It was not a reassuring smile. "That's an interesting word choice. Twelve people died because of drugs that Hartwell knew were dangerous. 'Tragic' suggests an accident. This wasn't an accident. It was a choice."

Diana's expression didn't change.

"I'm not sure why you're telling me this."

"Because you made the choice." The man sat down without being invited. "Not directly—you're too smart for that. But the shell companies that funded Hartwell's cover-up? They trace back to you. The lawyers who designed the strategy for discrediting the victims? They were on your payroll. The regulatory capture that kept investigations from going anywhere? Your lobbyists."

He leaned forward.

"You didn't kill those twelve people yourself. But you created the system that killed them. And now we're going to talk about consequences."

Diana had faced threats before.

Competitors who wanted to destroy her. Regulators who wanted to constrain her. Journalists who wanted to expose her. She had survived all of them through a combination of resources, lawyers, and the simple fact that people like her were rarely held accountable for anything.

But these two men were different.

They didn't want money. They didn't want influence. They didn't seem to want anything that Diana could provide.

They just wanted consequences.

"Who are you?" she asked.

"We're the people who noticed." The quiet one spoke for the first time. His voice was calm, measured, absolutely certain. "We're the people who saw the pattern. The connections. The way you've built an empire on the suffering of others."

"That's quite an accusation."

"It's quite a pattern." The talkative one pulled out a folder. Thick. Heavy. The kind of folder that suggested months of investigation. "Shell companies in the Caymans. Shadow investments in Malaysia. The way certain regulatory decisions always seem to favor your interests."

He set the folder on her desk.

"This is everything we know. And we know quite a lot."

Diana looked at the folder.

She didn't touch it.

"What do you want?"

"What we always want. Accountability. You've spent decades building a system that protects you from consequences. We're here to explain that the system has limits."

"And those limits are you?"

"Those limits are the line." The quiet one stepped forward. "The boundary between acceptable and unacceptable. You've been crossing it for years. Getting away with it. Believing you were untouchable."

He looked at her with eyes that had seen things Diana couldn't imagine.

"You're not untouchable. Nobody is."

Diana Cross had options.

She had lawyers who could tie any legal action up for years. She had connections in government who could make investigations disappear. She had resources that most nations would envy.

But looking at these two men, she understood something that her money and power couldn't change.

They didn't operate within the system she had learned to manipulate.

They operated outside it.

"If I refuse?" she asked. "If I call security right now and have you removed?"

The talkative one smiled.

"Then we leave. We go back to work. We continue building the case against you—not just Hartwell, but everything else. The real estate deals that displaced thousands of families. The media acquisitions that suppressed stories that hurt your interests. The pharmaceutical investments that prioritized profits over safety."

He stood.

"We're patient, Ms. Cross. We've been doing this for a long time. We can wait while you hide behind lawyers and lobbyists. We can wait while you pretend this isn't happening. We can wait until the case is so overwhelming that no amount of money can make it go away."

He headed for the door.

"Or you can cooperate now. Accept some consequences voluntarily. Make restitution to the people you've hurt. Demonstrate that even someone like you can face accountability."

He looked back.

"The choice is yours."

They left Diana Cross alone in her office, surrounded by the trappings of power that suddenly felt less substantial.

She looked at the folder on her desk.

She didn't open it.

But she didn't throw it away either.

Three days later, Diana Cross announced she was stepping down from her position as CEO of Cross Industries.

The announcement cited "personal reasons" and "a desire to spend more time with family." The business press speculated about health issues, romantic entanglements, behind-the-scenes power struggles.

No one guessed the truth.

A week after that, Cross Industries announced a $200 million fund for victims of pharmaceutical negligence. The fund would be administered by an independent board with no connection to the company.

Two weeks later, Diana Cross was seen meeting with federal prosecutors. The content of those meetings was never disclosed, but several ongoing investigations into corporate malfeasance suddenly acquired new momentum.

Three months after Justin and Erik's visit, Diana Cross pleaded guilty to securities fraud and paid a fine of $47 million. She received no prison time—prosecutors acknowledged her "substantial cooperation" in related investigations—but she was permanently barred from serving as an officer or director of any publicly traded company.

Her empire survived, diminished but functional.

She did not.

ETHICS COMMITTEE—CROSS OPERATION—ASSESSMENT

The Committee has reviewed the Cross operation and offers the following observations:

1. The operation achieved its stated objective (accountability for Diana Cross)

>

2. The operation was conducted through methods that we cannot fully document

>

3. The outcome—a powerful figure facing actual consequences for systemic harm—is unprecedented in our experience

Assessment: The line is becoming enforceable.

This is a new development. Previously, the line existed primarily as a concept—a boundary that individuals crossed at their peril, but that institutions and systems could ignore.

The Cross operation suggests that institutions are no longer immune.

Implications: Unknown. We are in new territory. The tools that Lampert and Block have developed—or acquired—allow them to challenge power at levels previously considered untouchable.

This is either extremely hopeful or extremely concerning.

We are not certain which.

Note from Gerald Morrison: I helped with this one. The financial patterns that connected Cross to Hartwell—I identified those. The shell company structures that proved her involvement—I mapped those.

This is what I've been working toward for twenty-three years. The ability to see patterns and have them matter. To notice things and have that noticing lead to change.

I know the risks. I know what I'm doing is unauthorized, possibly illegal, certainly career-ending if discovered.

But Diana Cross faced consequences today.

Twelve dead people received something like justice.

And Theodore seems to approve.

That's enough. That's more than enough.

Justin visited the families of the Hartwell victims after the settlement was announced.

He didn't introduce himself. Didn't explain who he was or what he had done. He simply appeared at community meetings, at memorial services, at the small gatherings where people tried to make sense of loss that should never have happened.

He listened to their stories.

He witnessed their grief.

And he made sure they knew that someone—somewhere—was paying attention.

"Will it bring them back?" one woman asked. Her daughter had been twenty-three years old. The youngest victim.

"No," Justin admitted.

"Then what's the point?"

He thought about the question.

"The point is that it matters," he said finally. "Not because consequences undo the harm. They don't. They can't. But because when someone crosses the line—when someone does what should never be done—there has to be a response."

"Why?"

"Because the alternative is acceptance. The alternative is a world where the powerful do whatever they want and the rest of us just… absorb it. Accept it. Pretend it's normal."

He looked at her.

"Your daughter's death wasn't normal. It was wrong. And the people who made it happen needed to know that wrong has consequences."

The woman studied him.

"I still hate them," she said.

"You should."

"I don't think I'll ever stop."

"You don't have to." Justin stood. "But maybe—maybe—the next Diana Cross will think twice. Maybe the next company will consider the human cost. Maybe somewhere, somehow, one fewer person will die because of what happened here."

"That's not enough."

"No. It's never enough." Justin smiled tiredly. "But it's something. And sometimes, something is all we have."

He left her with her grief, her anger, and the cold comfort of knowing that the line had been held.

It wasn't justice.

But it was a start.

CHAPTER 36

The Confrontation

They opened the door.

Alaric Voss sat behind his desk, watching them enter with the calm of a man who had been expecting this moment for years.

"Gentlemen," he said. "Please, sit down."

The office was exactly what Justin had expected: large, impressive, designed to intimidate. Floor-to-ceiling windows. A desk that looked like it had been carved from a single piece of wood. Bookshelves lined with texts that suggested brilliance and reminded visitors of their own inadequacy.

And in the corners: three men with weapons.

Justin catalogued the threats automatically. Three shooters, professional positioning, overlapping fields of fire. Erik would have seen the same thing.

But Erik wasn't looking at the security team.

Erik was looking at Voss.

"You know why we're here," Erik said.

It wasn't a question. His voice was flat—the voice Justin had learned to recognize as Erik at his most dangerous. Not angry. Not emotional. Simply present in a way that made the air feel heavier.

Voss raised an eyebrow.

"I have some theories."

"Marcus Hale."

"Ah." Voss steepled his fingers. "You've connected the dots."

"You arranged his death. You used him as a test subject. You wanted to understand how we respond to loss."

"I wanted to understand what you're made of." Voss leaned forward. "And I learned quite a bit. The way you processed grief—channeled it into focus rather than rage. The way you maintained operational discipline even while mourning a friend. Fascinating."

Justin felt something cold settle in his chest. He started to speak—

Erik held up a hand. Barely a gesture. But Justin stopped.

This was Erik's.

"You've spent three years studying us," Erik said. "Building models. Running tests. Trying to understand why we don't behave like your other subjects."

"That's correct."

"And what did you learn?"

Voss smiled—the smile of a professor pleased by a student's question.

"I learned that you represent an anomaly. A statistical outlier that my models can't adequately capture. You operate according to principles that defy rational self-interest. You make choices that no predictive framework can anticipate."

"And that bothers you."

"It interests me. There's a difference."

Erik moved closer to the desk. The security team tensed—hands shifting toward weapons, bodies ready to react.

"No," Erik said. "It bothers you. Because if you can't predict us, you can't control us. And control is the only language you understand."

Voss's smile flickered.

"You think you understand me."

"I know I do." Erik's voice remained flat. Calm. "You're not complicated, Dr. Voss. You're not mysterious. You're a man who discovered that human behavior follows patterns, and you built your entire worldview around that discovery."

"It's served me well."

"It's left you hollow." Erik sat down—uninvited, deliberately casual. "You've spent your career manipulating people. Moving them like pieces on a board. And somewhere along the way, you forgot that you're a piece too."

The silence stretched.

Justin watched his partner operate—really operate—in a way he rarely saw. Erik was usually the quiet one. The one who acted while Justin talked. The one who handled the physical while Justin handled the psychological.

But this was different.

This was Erik in his element. Not the violence—the understanding. Reading Voss the way he read rooms. Finding the gaps. Exploiting the weaknesses.

"You killed Marcus because you needed data," Erik continued. "You needed to see how we'd respond. But you missed the point of your own experiment."

"Did I?"

"You wanted to know what motivates us. What makes us keep going when rational analysis says we should stop. You thought the answer was somewhere in our psychology—some trauma, some ideology, some exploitable weakness."

Erik leaned forward.

"But the answer isn't psychological. It's ontological."

Voss blinked. "I'm sorry?"

"We don't do this because of what happened to us. We do it because of who we choose to be. Every day. Every operation. Every time we have the option to walk away and we don't."

He let that land.

"You can't model choice, Dr. Voss. Not real choice. You can model preferences and predict behaviors and analyze patterns. But the moment someone decides to be something other than what their circumstances made them—that moment is invisible to your systems."

For the first time, something shifted in Voss's expression. Not defeat—recognition. The look of a man encountering an idea he hadn't considered.

"You're more articulate than your file suggests," he said.

"My file was written by people who made the same mistake you did. They saw the quiet one. The weapon. The man who follows orders and asks questions later."

"And that's not accurate?"

"That's the mask." Erik's voice softened—barely. "I've worn it for a long time. It's useful. People underestimate the quiet one. They assume silence means absence—that if you're not talking, you're not thinking."

He stood.

"I've been thinking about you for three years, Dr. Voss. Since the first time we noticed the pattern—the tests, the manipulations, the careful probing of our vulnerabilities. I knew someone was watching. I knew they were intelligent. I knew they would eventually make themselves known."

"And what did you conclude?"

"That you're afraid." Erik's voice was almost gentle. "Not of us specifically. Of what we represent. The possibility that your entire framework is incomplete. That human beings contain something your models can't capture."

"Free will is a philosophical fiction."

"Free will is sitting down in your office with three guns pointed at me and telling you that you've wasted three years." Erik smiled—one of his rare, unsettling smiles. "If my behavior were predictable, would I be here?"

The phone in Justin's pocket buzzed.

He checked it: *Secondary location found. Rachel's tracker activated. Backup team en route. ETA 6 minutes.*

He looked at Erik. Erik looked at Voss.

"My colleague is going to show you something now," Erik said. "Financial records. Communication intercepts. Evidence. Your entire network, documented and ready for distribution."

Justin pulled out his phone. Showed Voss the screen.

Voss's face went pale.

"That's impossible. My security—"

"Focused on the wrong threats," Erik said. "You were so busy studying us that you missed the bureaucrat who was quietly building a case against you for two years. You missed the analyst who tracked your financial flows. You missed the network of people who wanted you stopped."

"Morrison."

"Morrison. And others. People you never noticed because they didn't fit your profile of a threat." Erik moved toward the door. "That's the thing about models, Dr. Voss. They're only as good as the assumptions you build them on. You assumed the threat would come from people like us—operatives, warriors, direct action."

He paused at the door.

"It came from the people who pay attention. Who notice patterns. Who write memos that no one reads until someone finally does."

The security team moved.

Erik had been waiting for it.

The first man went down before his weapon cleared the holster—a strike to the throat that ended the fight before it started. The second managed one shot that went wide before Erik's elbow found his temple.

The third was positioned well. Had a clear shot. Took it.

The bullet caught Erik in the side.

He didn't stop moving. Didn't slow down. Finished the third man with a joint lock that would require surgery to repair, then folded against the wall, hand pressed to his ribs, blood seeping through his fingers.

"Erik—"

"I'm fine." He wasn't fine. His breathing was labored. The wound was bleeding too fast. "Finish this."

Justin turned to Voss.

The man hadn't moved. Was still staring at the screens, watching his empire disintegrate in real time.

"Call off your people," Justin said. "Rachel Torres. Now."

Voss looked at him. Then at Erik, bleeding against the wall, still somehow radiating that terrifying calm.

"You knew," Voss said to Erik. "You knew they'd shoot."

"I knew one of them would get a round off. I calculated it."

"And you sat down anyway."

"Yes."

"Why?"

Erik's laugh was more of a cough—wet, painful.

"Because I chose to. Because that's what I do. Because you spent three years trying to understand us, and you still don't get it."

He met Voss's eyes.

"The line isn't something we hold. It's something we are. And you can't break what someone has chosen to become."

Voss picked up the phone. Dialed.

"Release her. Now."

He hung up without waiting for acknowledgment.

"They'll let her go," he said. "You have my word."

"Your word means nothing."

"No. It doesn't." Voss looked at his screens—the evidence of his exposure spreading across every channel they'd seeded. "But I have no reason to lie anymore. It's over. You've won."

Erik pushed himself off the wall. Took one step. Swayed.

Justin caught him.

"Hospital," he said.

"After we confirm—"

"Now, Erik." Justin's voice was firm. "Rachel will be fine. Gerald's team is already there. You're bleeding faster than you're talking, and that's saying something."

Erik almost smiled.

"I talked a lot tonight."

"You did. It was very impressive."

"I've been saving it up."

"I noticed." Justin helped him toward the door. "You can tell me about ontological frameworks in the ambulance."

They left Voss alone in his office, surrounded by the wreckage of everything he had built.

Behind them, Erik was bleeding.

Ahead of them, Rachel was waiting.

And somewhere in the building, the data that Gerald had compiled was spreading—law enforcement in fourteen countries, journalists at major publications, everyone who had ever wanted to see the line held against people who thought they were untouchable.

"Erik," Justin said as they reached the elevator.

"Yes?"

"That thing you said. About the mask. About people underestimating the quiet one."

"What about it?"

Justin pressed the button for the ground floor.

"I don't underestimate you. I never have."

Erik was quiet for a moment. Blood was still seeping through his fingers, but something in his expression softened.

"I know," he said. "That's why this works."

The elevator doors closed.

Outside, dawn was breaking.

And the line had held.

In the ambulance, Erik drifted in and out of consciousness.

"Stay with me," Justin said.

Erik's eyes focused. Unfocused. Focused again.

"The door," he murmured.

Justin went still.

"What about it?"

"Voss had files. In his office. I saw them while you were talking." Erik's voice was faint, medicated. "Project Threshold. Your door. He knew about it, Justin. He was trying to understand what it was."

"What did the files say?"

Erik's eyes closed. "Not what. Where." A pause. "There are more of them. The door isn't unique. It's a prototype."

"Erik—"

"We need to find them. Before someone else does."

The ambulance hit a bump. Erik's face contorted, then smoothed as the painkillers took hold.

"Later," Justin said. "We'll talk about it later."

"Promise?"

Justin looked at his partner—bleeding, half-conscious, still thinking about the work.

"I promise. When you're healed. We'll open every door there is."

Erik's mouth twitched.

"That's very philosophical for a man in an ambulance."

"I contain multitudes."

Erik closed his eyes.

Justin sat back and thought about doors. About prototypes. About what Voss had discovered, and what it might mean.

Some mysteries get solved.

Some doors get opened.

Just not today.

CHAPTER 37

The Reckoning

The aftermath of the Voss operation took three weeks to process.

Not the operational aftermath—that was handled in hours. The arrests, the asset seizures, the systematic dismantling of everything Voss had built. That part was routine. That part was what they did.

The personal aftermath took longer.

Justin found himself standing at Marcus Hale's grave again. Not because he had planned to visit, but because his feet had carried him there while his mind was elsewhere.

The headstone looked the same. Gray granite. Name and dates. A small American flag that someone replaced regularly, though Justin didn't know who.

"We got him," Justin said. The words felt inadequate. "The man who arranged your death. He's in custody. He'll spend the rest of his life in prison."

The grave didn't respond.

"It doesn't bring you back. I know that. It doesn't fix anything."

He paused.

"But it's something. It's accountability. It's consequences."

He looked at the sky.

"I don't know if that's enough. I don't know if anything is ever enough. But it's what we have."

He stood there for a long time, not speaking, not moving, just existing in a place where his friend was buried and his grief was allowed to be real.

Eventually, he walked away.

Erik was waiting at the car.

He didn't ask how Justin was doing. He didn't offer comfort or platitudes. He simply stood there, present, available, ready for whatever came next.

This was what partnership meant. Not words. Not sentiment. Just presence.

"The next one," Justin said, getting into the car.

"Already identified. Pharmaceutical company in New Jersey. Evidence of suppressed data. Twelve deaths attributed to side effects the company knew about and hid."

"When do we move?"

"When you're ready."

Justin looked at his partner.

"I'm ready now."

Erik started the car.

"Then let's go."

The pharmaceutical case was different.

Not harder, exactly. Not more dangerous. Just different.

The target was a company, not a person. A system, not an individual. The kind of slow-motion disaster that killed people through paperwork and neglect rather than violence and intention.

"Where do we even start?" Justin asked, reviewing the files in their hotel room. "There's no villain here. No single person to confront. Just a corporate culture that prioritized profit over safety."

"We start with the people who made the decisions," Erik said. "The executives who signed off on the suppressed data. The lawyers who designed the cover-up. The board members who knew and said nothing."

"That's a lot of people."

"Then we work systematically. One at a time. Until the structure collapses."

Justin nodded slowly.

"The line applies to institutions too," he said. "Not just individuals."

"The line applies to everyone who crosses it," Erik replied. "Regardless of how they organize themselves."

They started with the CEO.

His name was Richard Mercer, and he had been running Hartwell Pharmaceuticals for fifteen years. Under his leadership, the company had tripled in value. Shareholders loved him. Business magazines featured him. He was, by every conventional measure, a success.

He was also responsible for the deaths of twelve people who had trusted his company's medication to help them, not kill them.

Justin found him at his home in Connecticut—a sprawling estate that screamed wealth and whispered defensibility. Security cameras, motion sensors, a private security team that patrolled the grounds.

None of it mattered.

"Mr. Mercer," Justin said, appearing in his study at 11 PM. "We need to talk."

Mercer was behind his desk, reviewing documents. He looked up, startled, and reached for the phone.

"I wouldn't," Erik said, stepping out of the shadows by the window.

Mercer's hand stopped.

"Who are you? How did you get in here?"

"We're the people who know about the Renuvex data," Justin said. "The internal studies that showed cardiac risks. The deaths that were attributed to 'pre-existing conditions' and 'patient non-compliance.' The systematic effort to hide evidence that your product was killing people."

Mercer's face went pale.

"I don't know what you're talking about."

"You know exactly what I'm talking about." Justin sat down across from him. "I have 847 pages of documentation. Internal emails. Suppressed studies. Meeting minutes that show you personally authorized the cover-up."

He let that sink in.

"Here's what's going to happen. Tomorrow, you're going to call an emergency board meeting. You're going to announce a voluntary recall of Renuvex. You're going to issue a public statement acknowledging the risks. And you're going to resign, effective immediately."

Mercer stared at him.

"That's insane. The stock price alone—"

"Twelve people are dead, Mr. Mercer. Twelve people who trusted your company. Twelve people who had families, friends, lives that were cut short because you decided that profits mattered more than safety."

Justin leaned forward.

"The stock price is not my concern. Your shareholders are not my concern. My concern is accountability. My concern is making sure that the people responsible for those deaths face consequences."

"And if I refuse?"

Erik moved to the desk.

"Then the documentation goes public. Not through official channels—we don't trust official channels. Through journalists, regulators, every media outlet that has ever written about corporate malfeasance."

He looked at Mercer with the calm certainty of a man who had done this many times before.

"Your company will be destroyed. Your personal assets will be seized. You will spend the rest of your life in court, watching everything you've built disappear."

"Or," Justin said, "you can do the right thing. Recall the drug. Acknowledge the mistakes. Face the consequences with whatever dignity you have left."

Mercer's face hardened.

"I don't have a choice," he said finally.

"You have exactly the choice you gave those twelve people," Justin replied. "The choice to do the right thing, even when it's hard."

He stood.

"8 AM. Emergency board meeting. Don't be late."

They disappeared into the night.

The recall was announced the next day.

The resignation followed twenty-four hours later.

The lawsuits began within the week.

And slowly, painfully, the system began to work the way it was supposed to. Investigations were opened. Evidence was reviewed.

The people responsible for the deaths were held accountable through the legal process that should have caught them years earlier.

Justin watched the news coverage from another hotel room, in another city, preparing for another operation.

"It's not enough," he said.

Erik looked up from his laptop. "It never is."

"Twelve people are still dead. No amount of lawsuits or resignations changes that."

"No."

"So what's the point?"

Erik was quiet for a moment.

"The point is that the next company thinks twice. The next executive considers the consequences before signing off on a cover-up. The next time someone has to choose between profit and safety, they remember what happened to Hartwell Pharmaceuticals."

"Deterrence."

"Prevention. Or at least, the hope of prevention."

Justin nodded slowly.

"I don't know if it's enough," he said.

"It's not," Erik agreed. "But it's what we have. And tomorrow—"

"Tomorrow we do it again."

"Yes."

They sat in silence, two men in a hotel room, contemplating the endless work of trying to make things slightly better than they were.

It wasn't heroic.

It wasn't glamorous.

It wasn't even particularly satisfying.

But it was necessary.

And sometimes, necessary was all you could hope for.

CHAPTER 38

The Line Holds

Sarah Chen went home that week.

Not to Pennsylvania—to a new home, a new city. The third identity she'd had since her father died. But for the first time in years, she felt something like peace.

Justin found her before she left. He was waiting in the hospital hallway—he'd taken a bullet during the confrontation with Voss, nothing serious, but enough to require attention.

"Thank you," she said. "For what you did for my father. For what you did for his memory."

Justin shook his head. "We didn't save him."

"No. But you made sure his death meant something." She paused. "The fund you set up. The one for my education. I know it was you."

"I don't know what you're talking about."

Something flickered across Sarah's face—not quite a smile, but close.

"My father would have liked you," she said. "He believed in people who did the right thing even when it was hard."

"He was a good man."

"He was an accountant." The smile became real. "But he was brave when it mattered. And so are you."

She left.

Justin watched her go.

The next few weeks were cleanup.

Reports to file. Debriefings to attend. The endless bureaucracy that followed any operation, regardless of how unofficial it had been.

Gerald Morrison wrote seventeen memos about the Voss case. As usual, no one read them. As usual, he wrote them anyway.

The Ethics Committee issued a formal statement that managed to condemn and commend simultaneously—a masterpiece of bureaucratic ambiguity that satisfied no one and offended everyone.

Voss's trial was scheduled for the spring. His lawyers were already preparing appeals. The system would do what the system did—slowly, imperfectly, but eventually.

And Justin and Erik?

They went back to work.

The call came on a Tuesday.

A pharmaceutical company in New Jersey. Evidence of suppressed data. People dying from side effects that the company had known about and hidden.

Standard operation. Familiar territory.

Justin read the file and felt something he hadn't felt in weeks: purpose.

"Ready?" Erik asked.

"Always."

They moved out.

The pharmaceutical case took three weeks.

Criminal charges. Civil suits. A complete restructuring of leadership. Not their doing—not directly—but they had created the conditions. Provided the evidence. Applied the pressure that forced the system to work.

It wasn't justice.

Justice would require the impossible—undoing the harm, restoring the dead, repairing the trust that had been broken.

But it was accountability.

And accountability, they had learned, was sometimes the best you could hope for.

Justin found himself at Marcus's grave on a Sunday.

He didn't know why he'd come. He'd never been the type for cemetery visits, for conversations with the dead. But something had drawn him here—some need for closure, perhaps, or just the simple desire to stand in a place that Marcus had once stood.

"We got him," Justin said to the headstone. "Voss. We got him."

The stone didn't respond.

"I know it doesn't bring you back. I know it doesn't fix anything. But I wanted you to know."

He stood there for a while longer.

"The line held," he said finally. "That's what you always said was important. Not the victories, not the defeats—just whether the line held."

He looked up at the sky.

"It held, Marcus. It's still holding."

He turned and walked away.

Behind him, the grave sat silent in the afternoon light, marking a spot where a good man had been laid to rest, and where a promise had been kept.

That night, Justin and Erik sat on the roof of their safehouse.

It had become a habit—climbing up here when things got heavy, looking out at the city, saying the things that couldn't be said anywhere else.

"You ever think about stopping?" Justin asked.

Erik considered the question.

"No," he said finally.

"Never?"

"Never." Erik looked at him. "Do you?"

Justin let the silence stretch.

"Sometimes," he admitted. "When it gets hard. When we lose someone. When the weight of it feels like too much."

"But you don't stop."

"No. I don't."

"Why?"

Justin thought about it. Really thought about it—not the easy answer, not the principle, but the truth beneath.

"Because if I stop," he said, "then someone else doesn't get saved. Someone else's father dies for doing the right thing. Someone else's daughter grows up without them."

He looked at Erik.

"I can't save everyone. I know that. But every time I think about stopping, I think about the one person I might have saved if I kept going. And I can't let them down."

Erik nodded.

"That's why I don't think about stopping," he said. "It's easier to just… keep moving. Keep working. Keep holding the line."

"Is that healthy?"

Something shifted in Erik's expression.

"Probably not," he said. "But it's what we have."

They sat in silence for a while longer, watching the city lights.

"Tomorrow?" Justin asked.

"Tomorrow," Erik agreed.

They climbed down from the roof.

The work continued.

The line held.

And that was enough.

CHAPTER 39

The Cost

The bill always comes due.

Justin learned this early in his career—learned it in ways that left marks both visible and invisible. Every choice has consequences. Every action ripples outward, touching lives that you'll never know about, changing futures that you'll never see.

The work exacted a price.

And the price was always higher than you expected.

He was fifty-three years old when his hands first started shaking.

Not dramatically—not the tremor of an old man losing control of his body. Just a subtle vibration that appeared when he was tired, or stressed, or thinking too hard about things that couldn't be undone.

The doctors called it essential tremor. Benign, they said. Nothing to worry about.

Justin knew better.

The tremor was his body keeping score. Every fight, every injury, every moment of extreme stress—they accumulated. They compounded. And eventually, they demanded payment.

Erik noticed, of course.

Erik noticed everything.

"Your hands," he said one evening. They were in a hotel in Berlin, recovering from an operation that had gone well but felt hollow.

"I know."

"How long?"

"Six months. Maybe longer."

Erik was quiet.

"Does it affect your shooting?"

"Not yet."

"But it will."

Justin didn't answer. He didn't need to.

They had a conversation that night that they had been avoiding for years.

About the future. About what happened when the work was no longer possible. About the day—inevitable, approaching, unavoidable—when their bodies would fail them.

"We're not young anymore," Justin said. It was obvious, but saying it made it real.

"No."

"And this work—" He gestured at everything around them. The hotel room. The equipment. The accumulated evidence of decades of operations. "—it requires things that we won't always be able to give."

"What are you suggesting?"

"I'm not suggesting anything. I'm acknowledging reality."

Erik stood and walked to the window.

"I've thought about it," he admitted. "Stopping. Finding something else to do with whatever time I have left."

"And?"

"And I can't imagine it. Can't picture a life where I wake up without purpose. Without the knowledge that somewhere, something I could have stopped is happening because I chose to stay home."

Justin nodded.

"That's the cost," he said. "Not just what the work takes from us. But what we become without it."

They had never talked about retirement.

Not because it was morbid—they faced mortality regularly, in contexts far more immediate than aging. But because retirement implied a future that neither of them could quite believe in.

People like them didn't retire.

They just stopped.

"There's a succession problem," Justin said eventually.

Erik turned from the window.

"Meaning?"

"Meaning that when we're gone—really gone—who holds the line? Who does what we do?"

"Someone else."

"Who? We've spent decades developing skills that most people can't imagine. We've built networks, cultivated sources, created infrastructure. All of that disappears when we do."

Erik considered this.

"So we train someone."

"Who? Who could we possibly train? Who has the skills, the conviction, the willingness to sacrifice everything for principles that most people don't even understand?"

"We found each other."

"By accident. By luck. By circumstances that can't be replicated."

Justin stood and began pacing—a habit he had developed when thinking through difficult problems.

"The line doesn't die with us," he said. "It can't. Too many people depend on it. Too many systems rely on the knowledge that crossing certain boundaries has consequences."

"Then what do you propose?"

"I don't know." Justin stopped pacing. "But we need to figure it out. Before it's too late."

The answer, when it came, was not what either of them expected.

It came in the form of a young woman named Rachel Torres.

She had been an analyst—like Gerald, but younger, angrier, more willing to take risks. She had been fired for asking questions that her superiors didn't want asked. She had been blacklisted for writing reports that contradicted official narratives.

She was, in short, exactly the kind of person that the system was designed to destroy.

Justin found her in a bar in Washington, drinking alone, staring at a wall that wasn't going to give her any answers.

"Ms. Torres," he said, sitting down beside her. "I think we should talk."

The conversation lasted four hours.

Justin told her about the line. About the work. About the years of operations that had made him and Erik into whatever they were now.

Rachel listened.

She asked questions—sharp questions, probing questions, the kind of questions that revealed a mind that saw patterns and connections that others missed.

"Why me?" she asked finally.

"Because you notice things. Because you care about things that other people have decided not to care about. Because you got fired for telling the truth, and you're angry about it."

"I'm angry about a lot of things."

"Good. Anger is useful. But only if it's directed properly."

Justin looked at her.

"We're not offering you a job," he said. "We're offering you a purpose. A way to use your skills, your anger, your conviction—to do something that matters."

"And if I refuse?"

"Then you go back to your drink and your wall and your anger. And somewhere, someone who deserves consequences won't face them."

Rachel absorbed this.

"When do I start?" she asked.

The training took three years.

Not the physical training—Rachel was already capable, already skilled, already possessed of the kind of determination that couldn't be taught. But the mental training. The strategic training. The understanding of how to operate in a world that was more complex than most people realized.

Justin and Erik taught her everything they knew.

And slowly, carefully, she began to take on responsibilities.

Operations at first—simple ones, carefully supervised. Then more complex situations. Then, finally, independent work.

She was good.

Better than good.

She was, Justin realized, the future of the line.

"Do you think she's ready?" Erik asked one night.

They were watching Rachel run an operation—surveillance footage from a facility in Eastern Europe where she was conducting her first fully independent mission.

"As ready as anyone can be."

"That's not an answer."

"It's the only answer I have." Justin watched the screen. "She's skilled. She's committed. She understands the principles."

"But?"

"But understanding principles and living them are different things. She'll face moments where everything she believes is tested. Where the easy choice and the right choice diverge completely."

"Like we did."

"Like we still do."

On the screen, Rachel made a decision. A split-second choice that could have gone either way.

She chose correctly.

Justin allowed himself a small smile.

"She'll be fine," he said.

"And us?"

"We keep going. As long as we can. And when we can't—" He looked at Erik. "—we trust that we've done enough."

"Have we?"

Justin thought about the question.

He thought about all the operations. All the targets. All the lines held and consequences imposed and lives saved and lives lost.

"I don't know," he admitted. "But I know we tried. I know we gave everything we had. And I know that somewhere, right now, someone is alive because of what we did."

He turned back to the screen.

"That has to be enough. Because it's all we have."

ETHICS COMMITTEE—SUCCESSION PLANNING

The Committee has received reports that Agents Lampert and Block are engaged in some form of succession planning.

We do not know what this planning involves.

We have not been consulted.

We are choosing to interpret this as a positive development—an acknowledgment that the work must continue beyond any individual operatives.

Recommendation: Monitor the situation. Do not interfere.

Note: We have been monitoring and not interfering for years. We are not sure why we keep pretending that our recommendations matter.

But we keep making them anyway.

Because that's what we do.

Because the record matters.

Because someone has to notice.

CHAPTER 40

The Legacy

Five Years After Voss

The intelligence community called them ghosts.

Not because they were dead—though many people assumed they were, based on the operational silence that had descended over the past eighteen months. But because they had become something more than individuals. Something that existed in stories, in whispers, in the collective understanding of people who operated in dark corners of the world.

The Line.

It had taken on a life of its own.

Rachel Torres sat in a café in Lisbon, reading reports that didn't officially exist.

She had been doing this work for three years now—long enough to understand it, not long enough to become numb to it. Every file she read represented a choice. A decision about which problems were hers to solve and which weren't.

The line, she had learned, was not a fixed thing.

It moved. It shifted. It responded to circumstances in ways that Justin and Erik had tried to explain but that could only be truly understood through experience.

"You're thinking too hard," said a voice beside her.

Rachel looked up.

Justin Lampert sat down across from her, looking older than she remembered. The tremor in his hands was more pronounced now—visible without effort, a constant reminder that time caught up with everyone.

"I thought you were retired," Rachel said.

"I am." Justin smiled. "This is just coffee."

"Coffee in Lisbon. With active operational files spread across my table."

"Coincidence."

"There are no coincidences in this business. You taught me that."

Justin's smile faded slightly.

"I taught you a lot of things. Some of them were even true."

They talked for three hours.

Not about operations—Rachel had her own handlers now, her own network, her own infrastructure. The work had evolved, adapted, become something different from what Justin and Erik had built.

But the principles remained.

The line remained.

"How do you know?" Rachel asked finally. "When you've crossed it? When you've gone too far?"

Justin considered the question.

"You don't," he admitted. "Not always. Sometimes you're certain—absolutely certain—that you're doing the right thing. And you're wrong. And sometimes you're tormented by doubt, convinced that you've made a terrible mistake. And you're right."

"That's not very helpful."

"No. But it's honest." Justin leaned back in his chair. "The line isn't a calculation. It's not something you figure out through logic and analysis. It's something you feel. Something you know in your bones, even when your brain is telling you something different."

"Intuition?"

"Conscience." Justin looked at her with eyes that had seen too much and learned too little. "The line is your conscience, Rachel. The part of you that knows the difference between necessary and unforgivable. The part that refuses to accept that some things are acceptable just because other people accept them."

"And when your conscience is wrong?"

"Then you live with the consequences. You acknowledge the mistake. You try to do better next time." He smiled tiredly. "That's all any of us can do."

Erik arrived an hour later.

He looked better than Justin—still sharp, still alert, still possessed of the particular stillness that had always defined him.

The years had been kinder to him, physically at least.

"Rachel," he said, sitting down.

"Erik."

"The Munich operation. I read the report."

Rachel tensed. The Munich operation had been controversial—a decision she still wasn't sure about, a line that might have been crossed.

"And?"

"And you did well. Not perfectly—there's no such thing as perfectly. But well."

Rachel exhaled slowly.

"I wasn't sure. The target had connections that I didn't fully understand. The collateral damage was—"

"Minimal. And justified by the outcome." Erik looked at her with the calm certainty that she was still learning to develop. "You made a difficult choice. You made it quickly. You made it correctly. That's what matters."

"Is it? Sometimes I wonder if we're just telling ourselves stories. Justifying things that shouldn't be justified."

Erik was quiet for a moment.

"We are," he said finally. "That's what humans do. We create narratives that make sense of our choices. We construct meaning out of chaos."

"That sounds nihilistic."

"It's realistic. The question isn't whether we're telling ourselves stories. The question is whether the stories are true enough to guide us toward something better."

He looked at her.

"Are yours?"

Rachel thought about the question.

She thought about the operations she had run. The targets she had chosen. The people she had saved and the people she had failed to save.

"I think so," she said. "Most of the time."

"Most of the time is all any of us have."

They walked through Lisbon together—the three of them, the old guard and the new, talking about things that couldn't be discussed in any official setting.

Justin spoke about the early days. The mistakes they had made. The lessons they had learned.

Erik spoke about Anna. About the yellow parka he still wore on operations, thirty years later. About the way grief could be transformed into purpose if you were careful enough.

Rachel listened.

She was beginning to understand something that Justin and Erik had never explicitly taught her: the work wasn't just about skills or strategies or operational effectiveness. It was about continuity. About passing something forward. About ensuring that when they were gone, the line would remain.

"There will be others after you," Justin said, as if reading her thoughts. "People you'll train. People who'll carry the work forward when you can't anymore."

"I know."

"Don't make our mistakes. Don't wait until you're old and tired to think about succession. Start building now. Find people who have the potential. Invest in them."

"Like you invested in me?"

Justin smiled.

"We got lucky with you. Most people don't work out. Most people don't have what it takes."

"What does it take?"

"Everything," Erik said quietly. "The work takes everything. Your time. Your relationships. Your ability to live a normal life. And in return, it gives you—"

He stopped.

"What?" Rachel asked.

"Purpose. That's all. Just purpose.' Erik looked out at the city, at the millions of people living their lives without any idea of what happened in the shadows. "For some people, that's enough. For others, it's not nearly enough."

"Which are you?"

Erik didn't answer.

He didn't need to.

They parted ways at sunset.

Justin and Erik heading back to whatever quiet life they had built for themselves. Rachel heading toward the airport, toward the next operation, toward the endless work that would define the rest of her life.

"One more thing," Justin said, before they separated.

"Yes?"

"The doubts you're feeling. The questions about whether it's worth it, whether you're doing the right thing, whether the line even exists."

"Yes?"

"Don't lose them." Justin's voice was serious. "The doubts are what keep you human. The moment you stop questioning is the moment you become the thing you're fighting against."

Rachel nodded.

"I understand."

"I know you do." Justin smiled one last time. "That's why we chose you."

He walked away.

Rachel watched him go—this man who had spent decades doing the impossible, who had held a line that most people couldn't even see, who had changed the world in ways that would never be documented or acknowledged.

Then she turned and headed toward her plane.

The work was waiting.

The line was waiting.

And somewhere, someone was crossing it.

ETHICS COMMITTEE—FINAL ASSESSMENT

SUBJECT: The Lampert/Block Legacy

STATUS: Transferred

After decades of operations, Agents Lampert and Block have officially transitioned to inactive status. Their work continues through successor programs that the Committee does not fully understand and has been advised not to investigate.

Final observations:

1. The "line" they established has become an operational concept recognized across multiple agencies and jurisdictions

>

2. Their methods—unconventional, unauthorized, frequently concerning—have been studied and adapted by organizations worldwide

>

3. The principles they articulated—about accountability, about consequences, about the boundary between acceptable and unacceptable—have influenced a generation of operatives

Assessment: We have spent years documenting Lampert and Block's activities. We have written hundreds of memos, filed thousands of reports, raised countless concerns about their methods.

And in the end, we have to acknowledge something that we've been reluctant to admit:

They were right.

Not about everything. They made mistakes. They crossed lines that shouldn't have been crossed. They caused harm that can't be undone.

But the fundamental premise—that someone has to hold the line, that consequences must exist for those who cross it, that the system's failures require someone to fill the gap—that was correct.

They were right.

And the world is better for their work.

THE LINE

Book One: Where Responsibility Stops

EPILOGUE

Where Responsibility Stops

One Year Later

Vienna

The café served the best coffee Justin had ever tasted.

Erik sat across from him, not drinking coffee because Erik rarely drank anything in public. His hand moved unconsciously to his side—the scar tissue still pulled sometimes, a year later. A reminder of what the work cost.

"Gerald's retiring," Justin said.

Erik nodded. He had already seen the memo—Gerald's final memo, number 2,891, announcing his departure from government service after twenty-four years.

"He earned it."

"He's not happy about it." Justin stirred his coffee. "He wanted to keep going."

"The investigation came too close. If he hadn't left voluntarily—"

"I know." Justin sighed. "But he's safe. Portugal. New identity. Theodore adapting to the balcony life."

"Cats are adaptable."

"Unlike the rest of us."

Cascais, Portugal

Gerald Morrison woke at 5:47 AM, because his body had internalized the schedule over twenty-four years and didn't care that he no longer needed to keep it.

The sun was already warming the balcony. Theodore already there, stretched in a patch of light, utterly indifferent to the life-altering circumstances that had brought them to this small apartment overlooking the Atlantic.

Gerald made coffee. Portuguese coffee, which was different from American coffee in ways he was still cataloguing. Stronger.

Smaller cups. A ritual that required attention.

He sat on the balcony with his cup and watched the fishing boats head out.

He didn't miss the work.

That was the surprising thing. Twenty-four years of reading reports, identifying patterns, writing memos that no one read—he had expected withdrawal. Had expected the quiet to feel oppressive, the lack of purpose to gnaw at him.

Instead, he felt... light.

Not happy, exactly. Happiness seemed like too strong a word for a man who had seen what he'd seen, documented what he'd documented. But something adjacent to happy. Content, maybe. Settled.

The work was being done. That was what mattered.

Not by him anymore. But by people he had helped train, helped equip, helped believe in.

His secure tablet buzzed.

Gerald didn't technically have a secure tablet anymore. He had surrendered all classified materials when he left. Had gone through the debriefing process. Had signed the forms that acknowledged he was no longer authorized to access sensitive information.

But Justin had given him a device anyway. "Off the books," Justin had said. "For emergencies."

Gerald picked it up.

A message from Rachel: *New network identified. Thailand-Myanmar corridor. Scale is significant. Could use analytical support.*

Below that, a second message: *If you're bored.*

Gerald smiled.

He looked at Theodore. Theodore looked back with the particular disdain of a cat who had been interrupted mid-nap.

"Just one analysis," Gerald said. "Consulting basis. Nothing active."

Gerald opened the file.

Vienna

257

The news came through an hour after Gerald started reading.

A message from Rachel. She was running her own operation now—a trafficking network in Thailand, moving people across borders, destroying lives for profit. She'd been tracking them for three months.

She needed backup.

And she needed someone who understood patterns. Someone who could see connections that field operatives might miss. Someone who had spent twenty-four years learning to notice things.

"She's asking for Gerald," Justin said, reading the message.

"He's retired."

"He's bored." Justin smiled slightly. "And he's already running preliminary analysis. I can see him on the network."

Erik's expression didn't change, but something warmed in his eyes.

"Good."

"Good that he's helping?"

"Good that he can't stop." Erik stood. "None of us can. That's the point."

Cascais, Portugal—Three Hours Later

Gerald had found it.

The pattern Rachel had suspected but couldn't prove. A financial architecture linking the Thailand operation to something larger—a network of networks, new money flowing through old channels.

Someone was rebuilding.

Not Voss—Voss was in custody, awaiting trial, his empire dismantled. But the structures he had created, the pathways he had carved, the corruption he had normalized—those survived him.

Nature abhorred a vacuum. So did organized crime.

Gerald typed his analysis. Detailed. Thorough. The kind of work he'd been doing for twenty-four years, except now someone would actually read it.

Then he added a personal note:

Rachel—

The pattern extends beyond Thailand. This is a node in something larger. I recommend expanded surveillance on the financial channels I've identified.

Also: I'm not officially doing this. I'm retired. I'm watching fishing boats and drinking Portuguese coffee.

But if you need me, I'm here.

The line doesn't stop at borders. Neither do I.

— Gerald

P.S. Theodore says hello. He's lying, but I'm saying it anyway.

Vienna

"Thailand," Justin said.

Erik was already standing.

"When do we leave?"

"Tonight. Flight at seven."

"Rachel's running point?"

"Her operation. Her call."

Erik nodded. There was something in his expression that might have been pride—for Rachel, for what she'd become, for the line they were building together.

"She'll need local contacts," Erik said. "Sources who can verify the network structure before we move."

"I know. I was thinking about Elena Vasquez's approach. Building relationships with journalists in the region—"

Erik went still.

Justin stopped.

The silence lasted three seconds—long enough to matter.

"We talked about that," Erik said quietly.

"We did."

"You want to do it again."

"I want Rachel to know what's worked before. She makes the final call."

Erik didn't respond immediately.

"Elena's story ran," he said finally. "She's safe. If you judge by outcomes—"

"I don't."

"I know." Justin met his eyes. "And I don't have an answer for you. I don't know how to do this work without sometimes making choices for people who can't make them for themselves."

"The people we hunt say the same thing."

"Yes. They do." Justin walked to the window. "Maybe the only difference is that we're right and they're wrong. Maybe that's not enough of a difference."

Erik was quiet.

"Rachel makes the call," Justin said. "Her operation. Her rules. If she wants to do it differently, I'll support that."

"And if she doesn't?"

"Then you'll tell me I'm wrong, and I'll listen, and we'll keep having this argument."

Erik's mouth twitched.

"That could take a while."

"That's what partnership means. You keep arguing until the argument makes you better."

"Anna used to say something like that."

"She was usually right."

Erik's expression flickered—just for a moment.

"She was," he agreed.

He reached for the door.

"Erik."

"Yes?"

"How's the side?"

Erik's hand moved to the scar.

"It reminds me," he said. "That the work costs something. That it should cost something. That's how you know it matters."

He left.

Justin finished his coffee. Left a generous tip. Walked out into a Vienna afternoon that was beautiful in the way old cities are beautiful—layers of history, empires risen and fallen, and somehow, against all odds, something worth protecting still standing.

In Portugal, Gerald was analyzing patterns.

In Thailand, Rachel was preparing an operation.

In Vienna, two men were about to board a flight.

And somewhere in the machinery of the world, the people who thought they were untouchable were about to learn that the line was still being held.

THE LINE

will continue in

BOOK TWO: THE COST